THE OTHERWISE GIRL

The Otherwise Girl

KEITH CLAIRE

57607888

First published in Great Britain 1976 by Blond & Briggs Limited,
London and Tiptree, Colchester, Essex. Printed in Great Britain by The
Anchor Press Ltd., and bound by Wm. Brendon & Son Ltd., both of
Tiptree, Essex.

SBN 85634 052 9

Prologue

'No, do not get out of the car,' the man said to his companion. 'Let me begin by talking. And we can just look. It is always good to look.'

So they sat and regarded the village – the women shopping, the nondescript blotched dog that ran sideways, the sandy boy up on the farm-tractor. The street skirted Amberley Green, and led on beside and round the ancient church with its stubby tower. If you followed it, quite soon you would go out of the village again.

The man wore an old smeared sweater and old smeared slacks but he himself was not old. Perhaps he was just reaching his middle thirties. He had more authority than his companion for all the other's ample car and quietly styled suit. It was the man in the sweater who was the master and he took all his time. He brought out a sketch-book, he selected a pencil, a broad triangular pencil, but only to tap upon the open page.

'Do you see the Gift Shop? Twenty years ago, when I first came here, that was the only shop in the entire village. They've knocked two cottages into a supermarket now. And there's a new motel beyond the Rectory. Tawney would have hated it – had he lived this long. No – don't move. We will go on down to his studio a little later. We will go down and see where Tawney taught me so much, I promise you. But – everybody knows about that – even if it was a long time ago. You know about it. What you do not know about are the events on my very first visit here. I want to tell you that story. I have told no one before. Tawney himself did not know everything. We will stay in the car . . . out there is not the Amberley that I am going to tell you about.'

Yet his eyes drifted up and down the narrow street as if he were searching. All the while he spoke, he searched.

'It is beginning to rain. Now you will have to listen to me. It rains hard here. After a while you will see the thatch change colour with the wet. I will begin from the beginning in my own way. I remember it all. I even remember what my father said, before I left to come here. And what happened here still happens, for me. It happens over and over again in my head.'

I

'Good-bye boy,' my father had said. He had become un-expectedly serious for him. 'I think you may find it a bit strange down there, Matt. He'll be a bit different all on his own – in his own house, down there. Best of luck.'

After that I was taken up with the journey. I had started early in the morning and now it was night. The blunt long-distance coach growled on and on beneath high and shadowed hedges, the beams of its headlights thrusting at the dark ahead, a dark over a part of the country of which I knew nothing except the stories. Here and there I could make out banks of grass and groups of trees, once a pale house – all touched with a sudden ghastly headlight colour – and then the fingers of our lights rushed on elsewhere. I remember the other passengers only as pasty faces seated in their rows around me – lolling faces, sleeping faces. I can remember the driver's black back. I can remember the cat's eyes in the road staring at us from every curve, seeming to run towards us, only to fade to darkness underneath our wheels.

Yet I stayed so awake. I was fifteen and alone and full of suppressed excitement, I suppose. I knew that after so very many hours my stop was almost here. I had got two seats and my bag sat on one of them and I just stared and stared through my window out at the dancing shadows, at the passing hedges. I had to press my face against the window to see at all. Once, beyond the hedges, beyond the fields, I thought I saw a blacker motionless line that must have been the hills. I knew there were hills. Then our headlights picked up a lake, a sheet of water, and even as I took it in our lights had turned away and I had lost lake and hills and was looking at blackness, was seated all by myself in a coach and on my first trip to Amberley.

Tawney lived at Amberley.

You see, of all the people my father and mother knew (and there were lots of those – sometimes too many, I thought) the one I liked the best was Tawney. Tawney was the artist one. It was Tawney who lived in a barn down at Amberley, who sometimes visited us uninvited in London, slouching and sarcastic, and amusing Mum. He would take Dad off to the pub, just when lunch was ready; he would take me round exhibition galleries, he always knew everyone behind the scenes. Outings with him were always outings to unexpected places. And Tawney never minded talking to me for hours, explaining things and explaining how he saw things. For everywhere we went he had to make drawings, quick little sketches, tiny paintings: of the insides of machinery in power-stations, of the outsides of huge aircraft at the Airport (*he* could get permission for us to sit on a wing) or of people visiting the Zoo and from within the lion's cage. (We did not have the lion with us – only the smell.) I went with him when he did the wheeling traffic from the top of Marble Arch. And even if he did come up from the country he seemed to know almost everybody, the man selling long balloons down Oxford Street, the girl who sold him socks in Marks & Spencer – equally as well as the important museum officials and the Station Master at Paddington. Not that Tawney always said so much. He would often work in public places with a notice pinned to the back of his sweater: GO AWAY – CONFOUND YOU! And to me all he might say was: 'Hold this boy!' or: 'Get me some water, Matt. Where? How should I know?'

I would have to scurry round and ask strangers (which I did not much like doing) and find him his water. He would just sit on his folding stool in his grubby old slacks and with his tangle of grey hair, while his nervous clever pencil moved across his sheet of grey paper. I learned how he looked at things. I had to learn how he drew them. I had to draw them myself.

And now Tawney had asked me to stay. . . .

AMBERLEY 2 MILES, the signpost said, vanishing away behind me in the dark.

I still remember how the road dipped down to Amberley, how we went over a bridge and down and left and then hard left again, our brakes squealing, and then we were going under the bridge we had been over and down once more and yet Amberley was still below us, but for the first time I could see the lights of the village.

There were rather a lot of lights, a whole yellow glow was coming up over a line of roofs and trees. I had seen drawings of Amberley – Tawney used to do little sketches all over his letters to me. (I should have kept all those letters – but I never did.) I knew that the coach would pull up beside the Green. I knew that Tawney's barn was somewhere on the further side. In a few minutes – moments – I realised I would actually be seeing Tawney, Tawney standing feet apart and his hands pushed into his pockets, thinking of something somewhere different and yet still watching me and everyone from the corner of an eye.

The road narrowed sharply and we slowed and we were in light and this was the main street. All the houses seemed ablaze with light and then I realised that there were people everywhere. The whole village was awake, visited, cars parked head to tail – and then we were coming out beside the Green, pulling to a stop and there was actually a big crowd.

I stood up to see what was happening.

It was a midnight fair! There was the music of fiddles and a little drum, the playing of a pipe. There were the shouts of barkers, a row of stalls with flaring oil-lamps, people drinking, people shying at coconuts, a small roundabout, tents, marquees, people in funny hats, people waving streamers. Out in the middle of the Green there was a huge bonfire, yellow flames sparking and leaping against the darkness, and dancers. There were dancers in white masks and long cloaks and carrying tall torches, there must have been a dozen of them, stamping and turning in a great wide circle. The dancers were closing in towards the fire. . . .

Our driver slid a little wearily out of his seat.

'Amberley,' he said. 'One for Amberley.'

It pulled me up sharp. I suddenly realised that I really was arriving and I grabbed my bag and had to crab my way up towards the door. Even some of the other passengers were waking up, necks were being craned. Someone even found his camera.

'They do it every year,' the driver remarked, as if that explained something. 'Got any other luggage, boy?'

I hadn't. The driver opened the door for me, and then I dropped out of the warm coach and on to the road. The door slid shut, I stood back, and then, with a slight toot, the coach nosed out behind the crowd. For a moment I could only see its huge tail-lights glaring out like angry eyes, then one winked, and then the coach that had been my proper place all day had gone.

The night air was sharp, touched with the acridity of the smoke, the reek of strong cask cider and the unexpected billowing smell of freshly baked bread. For the first time I heard the crackling of that bonfire, and then . . . the shouting and the noises of the crowd just died away. I could really hear the shuffle of those dancers' feet, and then even the dancers stopped. A woman had begun to sing – I could not make out the words, yet what she sang seemed so far away and so sad that the whole of Amberley seemed to pause – everything seemed to stop and to listen. There was only this voice, the sputter of the fire and those torches.

It was at this exact moment that I realised that Tawney

was not here. There was so much to see, it was so unexpected, that I had not looked for him before. But then nobody had taken any notice of my coach. What coach? There was only me standing here now. I stood with my bag in the dark of a strange village and at the back of a crowd.

A slight sense of unwanted panic twisted a little in the pit of my stomach.

I supposed I could ask. But how many people in this crowd would know where Tawney's barn was anyway? Only a few of them could be locals. I wondered what I ought to do. The coach hadn't been . . . I looked at my watch. The coach certainly hadn't been early. And the driver had *said* Amberley.

I stood staring at the flickering light on the faces of the watching crowd. I could still hear the singing. I could not see the singer.

I hoped the driver had said Amberley. I would look a complete fool getting out at the wrong village at this time of night. At least I did know that Amberley did have a green. But perhaps they all had greens round here. It was at this moment that I realised that the village church was just behind me, that I was leaning against the low stone wall round the churchyard, that I could see the gravestones and a square tower hanging in the darkness. A notice-board! But of course.

I could just make it out: Amberley Parish Church. That was a relief. I decided that I had better wait here just a little longer.

My eye drifted back to the dancers. I could hardly hear the voice now, the dancers had restarted, somewhere in the background someone was playing a fiddle, the hooded dancers were turning on the spot. I remember staring, fascinated and puzzled by turn, still clutching at my bag.

'I think you must be Matt,' a girl's voice said in my ear.

I nearly fell over my bag. The girl was sitting on the

churchyard wall, she was almost beside me. She was just sitting up there, bare legs and bare feet dangling, short skirt and jersey. I could have sworn that she hadn't been up there before. I hadn't heard her climb up there. It wasn't easy to make out her face in the shadows.

'Yes – I'm Matt. How do you know?' I managed to say.

'And you're going to stay with Tawney – for a week?' It was a voice that half teased as it asked.

'That's right,' I agreed. At least, I decided, it did look as if I was expected.

I felt her hand grip my shoulder, she leaned forward and then dropped lightly down on to the road. She was hitching at her skirt, tucking in her jersey. I saw her face. She wrinkled her nose when she smiled and it was a nose with freckles on it – all her face had freckles on it.

'How do I know?' she asked and she was still teasing. I saw her tongue come out between her lips – almost as if it too had popped out to look round. I reckoned that she was almost my age, maybe a bit younger. It's hard to tell with girls.

'Well – everybody else is watching the dancing over there. And this is where the coach stops and you've got that bag with you. So you must be Matt – and you are!'

'Isn't Tawney coming then?' I asked. All along I had been picturing Tawney's joking, half contemptuous greeting.

'Expect he's working.'

She had turned her back to the fair and the dancers and I could hardly see her face for shadow. She was more interested in me – almost as if I was something out of a museum. She looked at what I wore, fingered my jacket, looked at my shoes, even lifted the bag to see how heavy it was. I did not know what to say.

'Sometimes,' she went on, 'Tawney doesn't know or care where he is – or even what day it is. But I like that. My mum goes to see him – though most of the village think he's mad. You know he mostly lives by himself now? But you don't have to worry – I think you're lucky – Tawney's a marvellous cook.'

I wasn't paying too much attention to what she said. Over her shoulder I could see that the dancing on the Green had stopped – no, not stopped, it was rather that they were somehow dancing by standing deadly still – and now a drum somewhere was giving a very slow beat, one and t-w-o, one and t-w-o, and then at last the dancers began to lift their feet to it with a sort of high stamp. I caught her eye, watching me watching them.

'Oh that – we do it every year at Amberley fair. Bit superstitious, I think. They say the harvest won't grow if they don't do it. Then they say they don't believe in it really. But they all get worried if they think it isn't going to be done. Been done for hundreds of years. I can do it!'

She began lifting her knees to the beat of the drum and she did it perfectly, though she was grinning at the same time.

'Did you hear the singing, just now? *She* dances in the last bit too – and that's the longest – all by herself. She's the one who runs it all and she's my mum. Come on – the last bit's just starting and it goes on for ever.'

I stared. I had never seen anything like it before, and now I knew that I wasn't lost I would have liked to have gone on watching it. But this girl had picked up my bag again . . . my hand had been grabbed.

'We go this way,' she told me.

We went.

We had no sooner turned our backs on the fair and the dancers than we were slipping through a little wicket-gate in the churchyard wall and were cutting along a path between the graves and into the dark. I could hardly see where we were going. There were the big shapes of the yew trees to one side of us and the squat tower of the church on the other. It was too cloudy for stars. Underfoot the path was slippery with moss and the white slabs and the battered crosses lay on either side.

15

'Walk behind me here,' she ordered, letting go of my hand. 'Path narrows. Hope you're not scarey. I still think I'm going to be scared – and then it makes me laugh. Steps down here – four of them.'

I let my feet find the steps first. It was more confusing than anything. I steadied myself on a big gravestone and wondered whose it was.

'You ought not to be carrying my stuff,' I complained.

'I know the way,' she replied. Her tone of voice indicated that she reckoned she could carry the bag with a good deal less trouble than I could. 'But I'll need your help down with it when we get to the ha-ha.'

'The what?' I asked, wondering if I had heard right. But my question got lost because we were going out through another gate that led down into a shadowy steep-sided lane. She had a warm hand. I had noticed that she made sure of taking hold of my hand again. It was even darker down here. I decided I might as well hold her hand as if I meant it.

'Who are you?' I asked into the darkness.

'Thought perhaps I wouldn't tell,' the voice teased. 'Then you would have to wonder about me all the way down to Tawney's barn. But that's not fair, is it? I suppose . . . I'm a bit like you now. I sort of visit Tawney sometimes. Oh, and my name's Chloe . . . well, I had to have a name, didn't I? C'mon, we go round here. If we cut across Mr. Bascombe's land and down over his ha-ha we save ourselves half a mile.'

I was really only certain about the last bit.

'What *is* a ha-ha? Is it a joke or are you meaning that it's really something else that you're not saying – Chloe?'

Chloe laughed.

'A ha-ha's a ha-ha! Mum's always called it a ha-ha and I've always called it a ha-ha. And Mr. Bascombe's got one. We'll get to it and then you'll know.'

We seemed to have come out of the village and were walking along under a hedge. I couldn't hear her bare feet, only the crunch of my own shoes. All at once I found that she was steering us off the road.

'Through the gap here,' she said in an undertone. 'And keep your voice down because we're on private land here, just behind his house. His ha-ha's on the far side. And if old Bascombe's dog comes – you leave him to me.'

That made me feel a bit uncomfortable. I didn't really know Chloe, yet I didn't want to not go with her. (I was lost without her now, anyway.) I wondered what we were letting ourselves in for.

'What sort of dog is it?' I whispered.

'It's a wolfhound – Irish wolfhound – lovely big thing,' came back. 'Bascombe lives alone – that's why he keeps it.'

I supposed it was all right. Actually a large part of me didn't think it was all right at all. I couldn't help feeling it was a little bit off to walk through somebody else's garden, even if it was the middle of the night. I also had a rather clear memory of myself when small and a neighbour's Great Dane had accidentally got into our flat and had chased me round and round and then up on to the kitchen table. It put me right off dogs too, that had, for a long time. I didn't like to admit that I was still rather wary of large dogs and from what I could remember Irish wolfhounds were just that. In fact if I hadn't been in front of Chloe I would have been glad to walk that extra half mile.

'I think I can hear it too,' Chloe was saying. 'Stand still a sec. I wonder if Bascombe's chained it up.'

I froze. I prayed that it was chained up. I prayed that Mr. Bascombe was on holiday and that neither he nor his dog were here at all. I remembered that Chloe was carrying my bag. We couldn't begin to run with that bag. I knew exactly what was inside it. And if we abandoned it, and if we did escape, we would have to admit what we had been up to, at least to Tawney, and I would never hear the end of it all week.

17

I stayed rooted to the spot. We were standing together, in complete darkness, in the middle of a lawn. There was an overpowering scent of wallflowers and my heart was banging in my ears.

A terrible baying sounded in the darkness. There was something particularly uncanny about that note because it seemed to come from every direction at once. I would not have known which direction to run to, yet I so wanted to run. Chloe's hand tightened a little. I felt hot and cold at the same time.

'Don't move,' Chloe whispered.

It must have got out from wherever it was. The baying got nearer and then I could hear the sound of a heavy dog bounding towards us from our right. I was only wishing that old Bascombe would come out and rescue us.

'Hello Paddy,' Chloe called, with a maddening calm. 'Paddy boy, here!'

She let go of my hand. She stepped forward.

'Paddy boy . . . come here!'

The hound stopped dead in its tracks in front of us. It must have seen her – heard her. I braced myself. Yet what was so astonishing was that the great baying gurgled down into a whimper. Its shadow twisted. . . .

The wolfhound was running away.

There was a scampering of feet off into the distance – and then an enormous silence.

I just stood there, feeling winded.

'Always the same,' Chloe was saying to me in a sad voice. 'He only ever runs away from me.' She sounded absurdly disappointed. I was thankful that she could not see my face. 'C'mon,' she said. 'He may have woken Bascombe.'

I was almost too choked with relief to speak. There were so many things to be relieved about. This man Bascombe coming out of the darkness to order us off would have been nothing. I did manage to pick up the bag and Chloe made no comment. We walked along, side by side. There was

18

lots more lawn. I was just beginning to decide that I could see a little further than I had thought when Chloe grabbed me by the wrist.

'Stop! Don't come any further for a minute. Must let me find the ha-ha first.'

I can remember being cross inside because she still hadn't told me what a ha-ha *was*. I could see Chloe going forward, and she seemed to be feeling for something with her foot, and then all at once she sat down in the grass.

'It's here,' Chloe said. 'Careful, if you come too far you'll go over. Sit by me, I'm on the edge. A ha-ha's a wall, but it's built down into a ditch so that it doesn't get in the way of the view. But we're on top of it, you see, so we've got to jump down. Then we're almost at the barn. I'll go first.'

Before I could reply she had launched herself forward and had disappeared. It was as if she had just jumped out of this world. I heard her land with a grunt and a breaking of sticks but I could not see the bottom. Then I could just make out her hands reaching up. I reckoned it was at least a six-foot drop or more. I lowered my bag down to her. Bag and hands vanished in the shadow. I felt oddly absurd, sitting up here, legs dangling, bag gone, Chloe gone, and me not even knowing where I was, except that I knew I sat on an edge – of a ha-ha!

'Jump,' said Chloe's voice.

So I jumped. I hoped I would land on my feet, I hoped I wouldn't turn an ankle, I seemed to fall endlessly.

I landed on Chloe. Chloe yelped and then there was the pair of us sprawling over each other in this rather damp bottom of a ha-ha. For an instant I could only lie with all the breath knocked out of me. I had the unreal feeling that I was not quite sure which were Chloe's arms and which were mine. At first I just lay, wondering if I was all right. Then I wondered if Chloe was all right. She was certainly warm. An insect ticked somewhere in the grass. Then I became alarmed because she seemed to be shaking all over – until I realised that she was laughing – in complete silence.

I asked her if she was okay.

'Me?' she asked between gasps. 'We might have killed each other!' And then she was laughing again. I found myself laughing too – I wasn't quite sure why. 'But are you all right?' she managed to get out. 'All my idiot fault. You couldn't possibly have seen me.'

She did not attempt to move. On second thoughts, perhaps she couldn't.

'I think I'm in one piece,' I announced, half crawling off her to find out. I was.

'Good thing you can't see me,' she was saying out of the darkness. 'Hair's full of leaves.'

I could hear her straightening herself. Then I discovered my bag by falling over it.

'C'mon,' she said. 'I'd better deliver you. Up this bank and we're in the lane again.'

I followed on her heels. It wasn't easy with my bag because even this side was quite steep. Then we did come out into the lane and everything was easier. We walked on a bit under the black trees. The lane rounded a corner and, almost at once, there was a building.

'Here we are,' Chloe told me. 'That's Tawney's barn. Go round to the other side and you'll find the door. You'll have to knock. He's never fitted a bell.'

'Aren't you coming too?'

For a moment she did not seem to want to answer.

'Won't want to see me,' she said, a little sadly.

'Oh!'

'Go on, Matt. He won't bite *you*.'

'Well – thanks for bringing me.'

She stood there in front of me as if she was going to make some reply, a shadow in the dark lane. All at once she leaned forward, kissed me on the cheek – and then she was gone. I was so surprised that I did not see which way she went. And there was no sound. I could not hear her. I supposed she was running barefoot along the roadside.

Again it was like . . . before I had ever seen her. It was silent and lonely. I turned away. I began to wonder if Tawney really was here. I carried my bag up towards the huge barn.

2

'Mind how you behave while you're there,' my father had said. 'Remember it will be his house you'll be in.'

At moments I was not certain as to whether I was walking on the path or on the garden. I seemed to stumble the longest way round before I actually found the door. It was so dark that I had to feel for the knocker with my hand. There was no knocker.

I knocked with my fist.

There was no answer.

Surely Tawney was not at the midnight fair and had missed the coach altogether? Or was Tawney asleep? I could see no light. A horrible sinking feeling came down all over me. Was this Tawney's barn even?

But then why should Chloe have brought me here?

The door had a handle. I twisted it somehow, not expecting it to open, and almost fell inside.

There was a very thick curtain just inside the door. This was no hay barn, anyway. I had to grope my way through the curtain. Then I had an enormous feeling of relief.

I was in one gigantic room. At the very furthest end there was just one small island of light. Tawney was sitting in the centre of it, his back towards me, a drawing-board on his knees. That was all I could see. What was he doing? Was he all right?

I drew a deep breath.

'Tawney,' I said.

Tawney did not hear.

I staggered forward, I barked my shin against something, I even dropped my bag. It was then that I realised how tired I was. I just stood there, my shin hurting like mad. At least I had made Tawney turn round.

The man revolved on his stern, though still crouching over the board on his knees. He sat peering out into the darkness where I was.

'Who are *you*?'

I felt almost too dopey to answer. I could only register that Tawney was as Tawney always seemed to be.

'Oh, you are the *you*! Blazes boy, it's old Matt and no other.' The man's voice was a growl but I was used to his growling. I even managed to grin, just listening to him. 'So I'm late, am I boy? That's it, is it? Working – that's what I'm still doing. Work's an illness, Matt. Mind you catch it. Never any cure – that's its whole beauty. But you – you found your own way here in the dark. My other friends all lose their's in the *light*! How, under the breath of heaven, did you get here?'

'Chloe brought me,' I managed to say. 'Didn't you know?'

'Who brought you? Chloe brought you?' Somehow Tawney found somewhere to put his drawing-board down in the shadows and got up on to his feet. He was a short and powerful man.

'That's right,' I agreed. 'She saw me after I got off the coach.' I remember yawning.

'Chloe brought you,' Tawney muttered, almost to himself. 'What would you have known about Chloe? But it would have been so like Chloe.' He looked up. 'You see boy – I told nobody that you were coming. Wasn't their business. Don't talk much when I'm working. But the village always talks. Your Chloe now? Tell me. Girl about your own age, yes? If I tell you that she had red hair, bare feet . . . liked her own way!'

It was like listening to someone talking a very long way away. I was very sleepy.

'I couldn't really see the colour of her hair,' I admitted, 'but that was her.'

Tawney strode away into the darkness of his barn. 'Just like you and me, boy,' he laughed. 'All cats have the same colour in a coal-cellar – with the light off!' There was a clicking of switches and the whole of Tawney's studio was ablaze with light.

When I could take my hands from my eyes I could see how big the barn was. Down one side there was a stretch of canvas nearly fifteen feet long, more like a piece of scenery for a stage than a picture. It was already half drawn . . . with dancers, dancers in white masks and long cloaks, carrying torches and with a high bonfire in the middle. I could see now whole racks of pictures at the other end, pictures stacked one against the other, and then a table littered with tubes of colour, dirty rags and two great pots full of brushes. There were sketches, photographs and posters pinned around the walls. (Tawney's posters – and photographs that had given Tawney ideas.) There was an unmade bed, a stack of newspapers on the floor and a towering bookcase stuffed with different coloured books. I had always imagined the barn to be something like this – but I had not realised that it would be so big.

'And with just one snap of the lights,' Tawney announced, 'just a cat becomes a red cat, a blue cat, a green or a white. You've never seen a green cat, have you boy? No, neither have I. But it did not stop me painting one once. Show you sometime, if ever I managed to find it. Now, what am I here to look for this time? Yes! Now tell me if you recognise this one? It was the red hair that fascinated me when doing it.'

I smiled. I could not help but wake up a little while watching, talking and listening to Tawney.

'Now you should be yelling at me for not being at your coach stop – and you'd be right – but to me I'm still in the middle of the afternoon.' He was pulling a picture out from the stack. Then he carried it over to a chair, had to lift off a box of chalks, three battered books and another old rag, before he could finally set his picture up. 'Come and look at red hair, Matt.' And then he was diving down into an immense portfolio and began rummaging in that.

I looked at this picture on the chair. I looked at it – and was jolted awake. For a moment I could not be sure if I was more startled by *how* Tawney had painted her – rather than *who* he had painted. I only knew what an awful lot I would have to learn before I could even begin to see . . . let alone draw or paint in the way that Tawney could. Yet I could see, that more marvellously than any photograph could have done, Tawney had captured. . . .

'That's Chloe!' I exclaimed.

Looking at his picture, at the slashes of browns and greens, the splurge of blue and all the different reds – they meant nothing – and then you blinked your eyes and they became Chloe standing. You looked down at her from above and there was this mass of red hair down her back. She was standing on a green river-bank in the sunshine and had only just come out of the water. She was twisting round and looking up at you over her shoulder, laughing and putting out her tongue. There were freckles all over her face, a blue towel in her hand. Yet she, the river, the towel and the river-bank, they were only tiny marks of different coloured paint, streak and spludge and spot.

'Never could get her to keep still,' Tawney was grumbling. 'Had to work from memory. Did it . . . did it for her mother originally. Somehow, the thing never got given. There was a reason. So it's still here. Look – this is Chloe too. Different! Hardly anybody knows I ever did that.'

He put a yellowing sheet of paper into my hand, not very large and rough at the edges. This was just a drawing. There was no colour. And yet it impelled my attention. I took the drawing in my hand. It was somehow cold and still.

There were no boldly blocked-in shapes, there was no sense

of movement here. The whole of this drawing was meant to be motionless and it was all done so delicately, with hardly more than a single outline by a perfectly controlled pencil. It was Chloe's face only, a Chloe drawn who did not move, who must surely have been asleep. The eyes were closed and the mouth unsmiling.

'That was Chloe,' Tawney said blankly. Then he looked back at his painting and nodded to himself. 'That's how she was. She used to do a lot of swimming. The drawing though, that should have been the last.'

He took his drawing back. I did not understand him. He stood there, swaying a little, staring at his own work. All at once he remembered that I was there.

'Er – want anything to eat boy – or drink? You put me off my stroke. But then of course . . . I should have met you myself.' He scratched the back of his tangled grey hair.

'I – I'd be quite happy just to go to bed,' I confessed. The mere thought brought back my yawns again.

'Hey! Of course you're tired. Would be! Who's chatting and yapping now? Show you to your room. *I* sleep down here.' He waved in the direction of the half-made bed. 'Don't expect you to. Guest rooms are up the ladder behind you. I'll take your bag. Up you go – hand over hand. Sure you don't want anything to drink?'

I was sure.

It was like climbing up into a ship.

It was a long high white room that Tawney had left me in. I suppose there were no pictures up there because all the walls sloped in with the roof of the barn. My bed was down one side, covered with a bright red blanket. There was an enormously long dressing-table and a row of built-in wardrobes. There was even a basin over in the far corner.

I dragged off my shirt and just let it drop on to the floor. I was deciding that I wouldn't be taking too long over washing. Yet I found that I was really too tired to be quick and that I was very dirty from falling down the ha-ha. So in fact I had to do rather a lot of washing. I have a memory of wearily leaning over that basin, at last cleaning my teeth, rather aware of a cool draught playing on my bare back and just thankful to be finishing. I swilled down the basin and finally turned round to bed.

Vaguely . . . I registered that my bed was neatly turned down. I had no memory of having laid out my pyjamas on the end. I saw my shirt hanging over the chair. I stopped!

Chloe was sitting on the dressing-table, her legs dangling, and she was still very grubby from falling down the ha-ha. She was busy brushing more leaves out of her hair . . . with my hair-brush. I suppose I was stupidly tired. Somehow I only seemed to be able to realise that Tawney had been quite right – her hair really was as red as that.

I remember her saying, 'This is the room I like staying in the most.' She seemed to say it to herself, not to me at all. She did not even look at me.

Somehow and illogically, I was not really surprised to see her – not today, not tonight. Everything was being so different today . . . but I was just too tired.

'What have you come for?' I found myself asking.

She did look at me then.

'It's my room really,' she told me. 'Like to come back and look at it sometimes. Came to see you too though. I've forgotten to ask you something.'

I blinked. Nobody seemed to want to let me go to bed.

'You'll see me,' Chloe said, 'on the Green tomorrow, in the morning, by the river. So you're coming out to look for me.'

It sounded more like telling me than asking me. Not that I was in any mood to argue.

'Yes – if you like – if Tawney doesn't want me.'

'He won't,' Chloe announced with conviction. 'He's

started a new picture. You'll be lucky if he even remembers you're here. But I shall remember.'

'Does Tawney know *you're* here?'

She shook her head and pointed. Behind me was my very open window.

'How did you get in?' I asked, not really understanding.

'Ladder perhaps,' Chloe said mysteriously. 'You don't have to look so worried. I won't kill myself. My mum doesn't know I'm here either. Going to say – I like those pyjamas. All those reds. Aren't you going to put them on, Matt? I've been admiring them ever since I put them out.'

I was not too sure that I would.

Chloe seemed to think this was funny.

'No? Look – I've another idea.'

In a flash she was off the dressing-table and had snatched up my new pyjamas. She was crouching – she was putting out her tongue.

'Tell you what – I'll give you your jacket back tomorrow, on the Green. How's that? You'll have to come out and look for me now.'

It came to me that I was being distinctly out-manoeuvred.

'Oy – give back,' I demanded.

I made to grab at her but she was all hands. Then she had jumped up on the bed and before I knew what was happening my own pyjama trousers were being thrust over my face. I couldn't see a thing. I was beating the air. I also seemed to be losing the pants I had on and Chloe was laughing.

I had to laugh too – in spite of myself. I backed away from her, grabbed at my pants, then managed to get my pyjama trousers off my ears. . . .

I was laughing all to myself.

Chloe had gone.

I supposed I just would have to go and look for her on the Green now. I supposed I would have to tell Tawney why as well. I went over to the big window and stared out into the dark. The night air was against my face and all I could see were the distant lights of the village. I had to admire the way Chloe had turned the tables on me. It was only after I had shut the window a bit that I began to wonder what she had done with the ladder.

3

Even before I opened my eyes I had that feeling of sunshine. A red of light glowed through my eyelids, was warm on my bare shoulder. I savoured the thought of where I was before I opened my eyes. I stretched out to the full and then my feet found that someone was sitting on the end of my bed. Cautiously, I withdrew my feet a little. My nose was being tickled by something soft!

I opened my eyes rather sharply.

I was staring upwards. Now I could see that I had a soaring ceiling of wide white painted boards sloping up on either side of me like a high white tent. My nose was being tickled by the end of a very long paint-brush. It was Tawney who was sitting on my bed – in an old yellow shirt.

'Cup of tea?' Tawney growled, without any smile, more like a threat than an offer.

I sat up, I smiled, tried to snatch the brush and was foiled. Tawney did smile. The whole bedroom was filled with so much sunshine because the sloping windows had no curtains. There was a great chatter of birds outside. I had slept well. Tawney had brought a tray, with a tea-pot and cups and biscuits. I lay there, taking it all in, hearing myself say good morning.

Tawney poured tea.

'Tell you what we're doing today,' he announced. 'All this morning – I am going to work. First thing – so are you. You sit still. Can you sit still? I'm starting my work on you.'

So there I was, sitting up – sipping tea when I thought I could get away with it; and there was Tawney running his pencil over a sheet of grey paper, snatching a gulp himself between strokes.

'After this,' Tawney continued, 'I'm cooking us a man-sized breakfast and then I am going to take a look at what you've been doing while we're eating it.' His head looked up from his grey paper. 'You brought some of your work with you?'

I nodded. I had promised to bring some of my own work and I had brought it – but I was not looking forward too much to what Tawney might say about it. People had been kind enough to say that I was quite good but Tawney was very much harder to impress. I knew that.

'I have brought . . . two of my sketch-books. I expect you'll tick me off about some of it.'

Tawney carried on drawing.

'I expect I will,' he said.

So I tried to sit still. All in a rush I was remembering I had to see Chloe this morning and wondered how I could ask.

'You don't have to sit all tight like that,' Tawney said suddenly, his paw sweeping out for his cup. '*You* ought to know that. And just drink your tea when you like to drink your tea, think like you like to think – and sit!'

I supposed that I should know – not that Tawney had ever tried to draw me before. I thought of Tawney's drawings of Chloe and wished that I could draw like that. I wondered what he would make of my things.

'After breakfast – and after I have ticked you off – you are not going to watch me draw, and I'm not going to watch you. Don't move! Don't mind you drinking your tea when you like as long as you don't move. After breakfast – you are not going to draw at all. You are going to walk round Amberley – looking. Looking, boy, because all drawing is looking – and then other people look at the marks your brain has made – because you have been looking. So looking will be your job today. But I shan't want you to draw what you see – not this time. Not yet. Meanwhile I am going to be

31

old and selfish and spend the morning getting on with my work. And then we'll meet at twelve for bread and cheese. How's that?'

I decided that this was a chance to put my tea-cup down. 'What do you want me to look at when I go round Amberley?'

'You'll find that out when I ask you afterwards – over lunch. But this I will tell you. Our skills – yours and mine – I'll tell you what most of my friends won't even admit.' He scratched his head with the end of his pencil. 'Drawing has become like riding and sailing. Sort of sport. No need for it now. Once the world needed so many people to draw and paint. It was the only way to give other people an idea as to what other things looked like. Then came the camera. That took the artist's bread and butter work away. But never despise photography, boy. No one can appreciate it more than we do – because we have been trained to look. Yet we can do things no photographer can imagine. Do you know what that is? We can take what we see and pour it through our minds before we let it out again – changed – much or little, but changed, Matt, by what we know and are.'

I ate a biscuit and wondered about eating another one. I remember wondering if I should be careful not to put myself off that man-sized breakfast.

Tawney, I reckoned, could make anything feel changed, simply by talking about it. When Tawney drew Chloe though – that wasn't Chloe herself – that was Tawney seeing Chloe. So what was Chloe herself? She had been right enough about Tawney. He was going to do his own work this morning and so it was going to be possible to see Chloe. And after all, wasn't Chloe herself a part of Amberley? I remembered that she was the reason why I was sitting up here without a pyjama jacket – she'd pinched it. All at once I realised that I ought to be answering Tawney. But the man had already gone back to drawing me. He hadn't noticed. He was working.

'Tawney – do we get changed too – by what we draw?'

For some moments the pencil went on moving relentlessly over the grey paper.

'Always,' he replied. 'And I'll tell you something else. So do other people – if they will only look.'

He went on working. I reached back for my tea and contrived to finish it.

'Tawney?'

The man did not seem to hear.

'Tawney, does Chloe come here often?'

The pencil stopped then. But Tawney did not look up – rather more down.

'She used to be here – very often.'

'But not now?'

'I do still see her here,' he admitted, 'but only sometimes.'

It was a glorious morning.

Tawney had stood over me and he had made quite certain that I did not take even my smallest sketch-book, and not even a pencil-end.

'I can tell you too that the village shop won't sell you a pencil either – on my orders.'

I wondered what Tawney had told them. After all, they did not know me. It was going to be a bit hard if another strange boy went in the shop today. It was a bit hard on me. I had thought that Tawney had said that nobody in the village even knew about my arrival. Not that I was worried. Tawney had almost run back to his work. I crunched away down the path and on to the road. I could walk comfortably round to the village and not through old Bascombe's garden. This time I would at least be able to see where I was going.

It was still quite early. Tawney had in fact got us up very early. The air had a sparkle to it, the hedges rose high and green on either side and there was a lot of chirrup from the birds. Down here, oddly enough, I could not see the village at all. A small stream was running by the road, bubbling and

jollying over stones. In the distance I heard a bell striking –
it was the clock on the Amberley church tower – the bell
chiming over the fields.

Tawney had looked at all my drawings in both my sketch-
books. All along – ever since it had been suggested that I
should come – it had been a bit alarming as to what Tawney
would say about them. But then I had also been afraid that
there wouldn't have been enough to show him. It had been
his suggestion that I should try to do some on my own. He
had teased me into drawing with him when we had gone
out together on his visits and had taught me a bit. At least . . .
he had taught me to enjoy it. So Tawney had sat munching
toast – to my surprise breakfast was served on a smart white
table-cloth, in spite of the mess in the rest of the barn – and
seemed to be able to look at both sketch-books at one and
the same time.

One was used to Tawney looking at things upside-down,
or sideways, or with only one eye. He had told me some of
the things he had wanted me to do: a milk bottle; and then
the same milk bottle with a rose stuck in it; three walnuts;
and those same three walnuts with a clean white handkerchief
spread over them; the view from my bedroom window at
night; exactly the same view the next day; the budgerigar
cage without the budgerigar. . . .

'They don't sound too exciting, boy – but oh, you will find
them difficult. You'll hate me for giving 'em and that'll be
fine. You'll be supposed to hate me.'

He was right. I hated him most satisfactorily. But I didn't
have the face not to try. I knew I was coming down to see
him – and I liked him. I found I didn't get bored. (My dad
thought I wouldn't stick at it!) I went through a stage of
getting swell-headed about my efforts. But in front of
Tawney I was petrified!

First of all Tawney said nothing. He did wrinkle up his
nose at everything – but then Tawney was always wrinkling

up that nose. He did not even tick me off when he came to it. He even grinned.

'Got a nasty feeling, Matt – you might almost have enjoyed yourself doing some of this. Have to put a stop to that. That's why your next job's thinking about what you might draw, in Amberley, and telling me your reason. Might even ask you to remember it – for a start. Want you to spend the morning drawing without doing any drawing. Asking you to move an imaginary pencil in your real head.'

He wouldn't say if anything I had done was either good or bad.

My road took a steep slope down and at the bottom the stream emptied into a pond at the end of a field while the road itself swung away round a blind corner. I supposed I must have walked right by Bascombe's land. There were geese on the pond. I stood there, watching them in an idle sort of way. After all, wasn't I supposed to stop and watch?

The surface of the pond was not like the stream – it was glass-still. The geese, grey-necked and dark-winged, just floated on green water without seeming to do anything at all. The field beyond them stretched away and away towards a wood. Flies buzzed up at my face and I could taste the smell of cow.

A bicycle bell shrilled sharply!

I jumped – almost the wrong way.

A man in a dapper dark suit, bushing eyebrows and a rector's dog-collar, a tall man astride a tall bicycle that still seemed a size too small, was pedalling madly down towards me. It was one of those old-fashioned bikes with a basket on the front just like a butcher's boy. It was a full basket.

'Helloooo Maaatt!' a huge hollow voice shouted as the man negotiated both curve and me at an alarming angle, his knees pumping up and down as he charged the further slope.

I stared at his now retreating back. I was obviously no secret in Amberley. I marched on up the hill the other way, wondering what it was I was going to see.

Round and up and between more trees and I was passing cottages that seemed weighed down into the ground by the thatch upon their roofs. My lane narrowed and I saw other cottages higher up on a bank behind. Then I was passing the churchyard again and even with the sun it was dark with its trees. Just ahead was the Green.

Nobody much seemed to be about. I saw the remains of last night's fair – the empty booths and stalls, the round circle of white ash where the bonfire had been. I paused before crossing the road to let a Post Office van go by. The postman waved.

Can't be me, I thought – but there was no one else.

Tawney had certainly disarmed me. Without my sketch-book, pencils or charcoal, I could not just sit down with all my paraphernalia and let the world know that I was a budding artist, that Mr. Tawney himself was teaching me and that anyway I was rather good. I just had to do real work. I had to look.

I wondered which way to go. Chloe could hardly have arrived. I decided that I would at least find my way round the Green so I set off across it. Amberley village only seemed to go halfway round. It just seemed to be countryside beyond. I looked back. There were the hills down which the coach had come. It was only when I had walked quite a little way that I saw the river on the Green's further side. I stopped and looked back again. The village houses looked almost like toys. I decided that I might as well walk down to the river. I wondered where Chloe would find me – or I would find Chloe.

Someone was picking marigolds along the river-bank, armfuls of marigolds. Even from this distance I could see that it was not Chloe. It was a woman . . . a middle-aged woman with streaky iron-grey hair, moving slowly, picking as she went. I remember that she had a yellow blouse on and that it was a different yellow to the marigolds. I watched her as I walked. She was picking her way towards me, bent over among the flowers, not looking up.

I wondered if I had arrived at a good place to stop. I was where the river arrived beside the Green. Perhaps this was where Chloe meant. Or should I just go on? There was no pressing other reason to do anything in particular. Somehow I simply went on walking.

As I approached, the woman straightened her back. I found myself drawing in a breath. I knew that in the country every-body said good morning. She looked at me very fair and square. I wondered if it should be me who ought to speak first. Was she waiting for me to say it?

I wasn't given any opportunity.

'Oh, Matt dear, will you take these from me, so that I can come up the bank?'

She spoke as if she had always known me. It was a tone of voice that one couldn't really question. I went down the bank and took the heap of flowers from her. She still showed traces in her grey hair that it had once been red. Her face had lots of little lines and tiny freckles and she was smiling up at me.

' . . . suppose he didn't remember to tell you?'

'Tell me?' I heard myself ask, still taken aback and not quite grasping what she was talking about.

'He was supposed to warn you against swimming in the Amberley river. Oh, it's so obvious he forgot. And shouldn't you at least have brought a pencil and paper with you?'

'Er – Tawney – Mr. Tawney – he said I could only go out and *look*, to begin with.'

She could certainly grasp what I was talking about.

'Oh yes, Matt. He would. That is exactly . . . Tawney. He is – was – I suppose you could say – he's a very old friend of mine. But he will forget what's important. So I shall have to ask you to promise me – I know it is a warm day – promise me you won't slide off to have a swim.'

37

She was still smiling but I could see that she did mean what she said.

'Why no,' I assured her. 'I haven't got any things, have I?'

The woman nodded, directed that we climb the bank, gripped my shoulder and came up with me. At the top I gave her the marigolds back.

'Our little river has this strong current that never ceases,' she told me. 'And then there are the weeds. Weeds catch your feet, current pulls you down. I only tell you . . . a girl was lost in this river like that.'

I nodded. I rather wondered who this woman was.

'I always collect marigolds at this time of year, while they are at their best. They are to remember her by, because she liked them so much. I enjoy remembering her – but that doesn't mean to say I want to have to collect them for you too. You see, you might not realise how powerful our river is. It comes down over a weir – that's the reason. The awful thing was . . . it should never have happened . . . she knew our river so well.'

'Where – where is the weir?' I asked, feeling that this might change the subject a little.

'See our hills at the back? Then those two higher ones – in the middle?'

She pointed, a bunch of marigolds still in her pointing hand.

'Down here we call them the Amberley Mounds, because that's what they look like. But when you get up there you find that they are a plateau really. The edge of the Amberley Moor. It goes on for miles – mostly sheep with a forest down the centre, where the river runs. The weir is on the edge. It's a marvellous sight, Matt – all that water flowing over the lip of the weir. You can stand on a narrow wooden footbridge right above it and watch the river pour and pour down between the rocks beneath your feet. Tawney did a whole series of paintings of it once – but he won't go there nowadays.'

38

'I'm staying at his barn,' I said. 'I've seen a lot of his work there.'

'His barn? Yes – I was the one who found that for him, originally. He so wanted . . . it was so important for him to have his own place where he could do his work in peace. At first, we had a cottage by the Rectory. Then we had that barn turned into his studio. It was perfect for him then. . . .'

The woman looked up from her remembering.

'I've been in Amberley a very long time,' she told me.

There was a silence.

'Then – then you must know why they dance on Amberley Green?'

'Oh – so you've heard of that, have you? You haven't seen us dancing, I suppose?'

'Yes, I have. I watched last night when I got off the coach. But only for a moment because . . . afterwards somebody told me it was a superstition. Why do you think they do it?'

'So you *did* see some of it. I was dancing myself. It's not what I call a superstition. We do it, because it has always been done. There's a rightness about it. It marks the year. It gives a shape to life, like saying good morning and good-bye. It's what was done and is done and shall be done. That is a good thing. I can remember being taught the dances, Matt, by my old Gran. She knew how it should be done, even when she could hardly drag one foot in front of the other herself. But I remember her old eyes glittering while she taught me, and her fist beating out the time . . . and I learnt all the songs from her, in the old words. Gran used to sing as if her heart was going to overflow. So sad they were, you see. My mother used to teach me too, but in quite a different way, usually when we were doing something between us and at some unexpected time. Yet when my mother sang those songs – then they seemed more angry than sad. But brave too. . . . Sometimes, I sing them like that.'

All at once she turned away. She put her marigolds over her other arm.

'You won't swim, will you Matt? Now these days, I don't go down to Tawney's very much, but I expect we shall see each other again. You can . . . give Tawney my regards. Enjoy your stay with him. Tell him to send you across to me – I'll sing you some of the songs as they should be, as they used to be, and as they're going to be. And you must show me your drawings.'

She was walking away. I did not even have a chance to thank her. It was afterwards I realised that she had been calling me by my name and yet had not once mentioned who she was.

4

The river curved away from the Green and through broad water meadows. There was a stile and I half climbed over and then sat there, looking back towards the village. I could just make out a huge fuel tanker edging its length cautiously round the church, the sun flashing for an instant on its curved windscreen as it turned.

The sun was warmer now. The only person that I could see was the woman carrying her flowers and now only a dot on the far side of the Green. I remember deciding to explore the church on my way back. Churches could have marvellous carvings, gargoyles, tombs and banners. Tawney was bound to ask me questions about it. (Good place to draw if it rained.)

Across the river an old dappled cart-horse was getting down to some serious eating, its white mane flopped forward between its ears, its long face with the blue spottings on its nose slightly on one side as it cropped the long grass. I watched the line of its neck as it moved – and the heavy white fetlocks were like great muffs above the giant hooves. The horse took its time, lifting its head now and then to shake away the black persistent flies.

It was a chance to get on with some looking. I wondered if the village shop really would refuse to sell me a pencil. But then everyone, just everyone, did seem to know who I was.

From somewhere behind me there was a splashing in the river. I watched a blue dragonfly planing over the reeds. Glancing back I realised that somebody else must be swimming even though I could not see them from this stile. There was a bend in the river just here. Perhaps if I went on I would see who it was. It gave me a moment of purpose. I swung a leg over and walked on round the path.

The river widened at the bend. There were high clumps of reeds and bulrushes but in one or two places the bank did slope down gently with grass and marigolds. I stood there, partly drugged with the warmth of the sun and not really surprised to see that the swimmer was Chloe.

The girl had not noticed me for she was wading out of the river on the further side. Yet there was no doubt that she was Chloe, even if she had tied up her hair and was still waist-deep in the water in a black swimsuit. I was almost treading on her bundled clothes, in a blue towel with white stripes . . . and right in the middle and neatly rolled: my scarlet pyjama jacket. I stood still, wondering what she was doing and watching her.

It was the cart-horse. Chloe was scrambling up the opposite bank, water running off her, a huge handful of grass in her fist.

'Sam!' her voice called high above the water. 'Sam, Sam! Come on Samuel – you know me.'

I could see the cart-horse. It was raising its head at her call.

'Sam! Sam!'

She was plunging towards the cart-horse out of the rushes. Then all at once it had seen her. To my surprise its ears went back, it snorted and with a whirl of heavy hooves it had turned about, I saw earth flying in the air, and with a clumping gallop it was away. Chloe was left standing, left holding her grass and rather forlorn. From where I stood, rather higher than Chloe, I could see that the cart-horse was still running.

'O-o-oh!' Chloe wailed. I could hear it from my side.

I opened my mouth to speak, and then closed it. Should I call over to her – or should I wait? I stepped back a pace or two to be out of sight behind the taller rushes. But then I could not see Chloe either. She was still gazing sadly after the horse.

'Hi! C-h-l-o-e!'

She turned about at that, saw me at once, dropped her grass and waved. Her face burst into smiles.

'Hello! You are early! Didn't 'spect you yet. I'll come back over.'

'Tawney gets up so early,' I was shouting in explanation.

But already she was splashing down into the water, half tumbling, half wading through weed, then breaking into half a dozen powerful strokes and then wading again. I saw how she kept her head well up to avoid wetting her hair. I went down and held out a hand for her that she obviously did not really need but did take. She splashed out and stood in front of me shaking a strand of weed off one foot. There was another bit that she was perfectly capable of removing but I took it off for her.

'I've been told what a dangerous river this is,' I teased. I also went and fetched her towel.

'It's not dangerous here,' she said scornfully. 'Nobody could drown here. It's further upstream that you have to look out, where there's a weir. Going over that isn't so funny.'

I handed her the blue towel. She liked being looked after.

'What made the horse bolt?' I asked.

'Oh, the horse.' She began to dry her shoulders. 'Did you see it then? I once knew a horse who used to let me do anything with him. I even used to ride round the field on him. Of course you did rather have to do the splits. D'you know, I remember, ages ago, creeping out one night and riding him round in the dark – just for a dare with myself.'

It wasn't difficult to imagine.

'Would you,' I asked, 'would you have ridden him just now – if he had let you?'

'Might have. Came for a swim really – before meeting you. But I'm so glad you have come so early. We can have a gorgeous morning. Hey, d'you want to come in for a swim? I'll come in again.'

I hadn't really expected that. For an instant I found myself calculating that it probably was quite dangerous unless you really knew what you were doing, and I might not show up too well in front of Chloe, who was probably a very good swimmer (so many girls were) and anyway. . . .

'I haven't brought any things with me,' I pointed out.

'Who cares? There's nobody around. Here – let's go and have a look.'

She was climbing up the bank and actually looking too.

'But I've got no towel,' I protested.

'You can sit in the sun. I've done that before now. And there isn't anybody about. Come on in with me, it's so lonely doing things on one's own always.' She had thrown her towel down and was making back to the water.

I stood there, remembering the grey-haired woman picking all those marigolds. There were marigolds everywhere.

'Aren't you coming?' Chloe was asking me over her shoulder. She was already paddling in.

It was hot, I told myself. I had to decide, I told myself. I knew already that I was shy, and shy because I wasn't confident. So I just went stubborn all over.

'No,' I said.

So there she stood in the water, knee-deep. There was a strong current flowing too, I could see that. I could also see that I had hurt her a bit and I hadn't wanted to hurt her. After all there couldn't be much danger because there were the two of us here. I wondered if perhaps I ought to go in with her.

'I've also come out here because Tawney sent me,' I said out loud. It must have sounded a bit hollow. 'You never said we were going to swim.'

'Didn't know then,' Chloe pointed out. 'You could always dry on your pyjama jacket.'

'But what were we going to do this morning?' I was changing the subject. Deliberately, I bent down and rescued

44

my jacket from the middle of her things. She watched me doing it.

'I only wanted to talk ... really. I feel so lonely by myself. And I like Tawney and you like Tawney and so I thought we would have things to talk about. There were never many people in the village who liked to talk to him seriously – not about what he does. He says you even draw a bit. I – I can't much – but I feel at home with people who do – and don't laugh at it.'

To my relief she was coming out of the water. She was picking up her towel again. She even wanted to talk about things I knew rather than me doing things she knew. And then – seeing her stand like that on the river bank – all at once I knew exactly where I had seen her just like that before.

'You should never give up trying to draw,' I told her. 'Most people can learn.' (I was echoing Tawney there.) 'That's why I'm supposed to be walking round Amberley and just looking at it this morning. Tawney believes in looking at everything first. But you must know that. Couldn't you take me round? You must know what there really is to see.'

She was standing on one leg and had put a hand on my shoulder to steady herself while she dried her left foot. Suddenly she managed to become both pleased and doubtful at the same time. She over-balanced and put her foot down again a little unexpectedly.

'Of course I know. But me take you round Amberley? In the daytime? Now?'

'Yes,' I said, wondering why she should find this difficult.

'Suppose I could,' she admitted, as if it took a lot of thinking about. 'Be rather a dare. You see –' she looked up – 'I don't go to the village all that much.'

'I – I thought you lived there.'

She changed feet and I had to stand firm again.

'I come from – well, it's further over really, now.'

My face was very close to the red hair.

45

'Yet it must have been here that Tawney painted you,' I pointed out.

She stopped her drying.

'He's shown that to you?'

There was a note in her voice that almost suggested that it was extraordinary that Tawney should have shown it at all.

'Yes. He showed it to me. I think it's marvellous!'

She looked at me patiently, as if she had heard all this before.

'He can make anything look marvellous,' she said slowly. 'That's just what Tawney does. No – he didn't really paint me here. He just sort of did sketches and the painting itself he did back at the barn. D'you think it's me though?'

'Of course it's you. It *is* you. He couldn't have begun to do it if you weren't the way you are. Wish I could begin to capture what he manages to capture. I'd love to be able to work like him.'

'But d'you think I'm marvellous?' She sounded both serious and curious at the same time, as if she had never thought about the possibility before and really wanted to know.

'A picture only grabs half a split second,' I told her. (That was Tawney again.) 'But it's you that's all-round, all-alive and all-real. You're what it's all about. No picture is as good as you are yourself.'

Yet Chloe didn't seem to be convinced.

'People used to visit his barn and look much more at my pictures than at me. And Tawney was so bad-tempered when he did this one. Everything was wrong and was my fault. I had to stand *here*. Well – almost – no, there, just beyond where you're standing. And he wouldn't even let me dry.'

She jumped down the bank to the correct place, twisted herself round and looked back up at me. She even held the towel just as she had in her picture.

'He made me stand still for ages.'

'You had your hair down,' I pointed out.

She nodded. I seemed to have done the right thing by remembering. It was as if it proved to her that I really had been struck by Tawney's picture of her. She tugged at the blue headband round her hair and shook it back.

Looking at her, I had to admit to myself that it was also Tawney who I was admiring now.

'That's it,' I said to her. 'But you've got to move a bit more round.'

She did move round, just as I directed. She stood absolutely right – only then she put her tongue out.

'You order me around like Tawney,' she accused, but she was laughing. All at once she was up beside me and scrabbling among her clothes. A comb came out of the middle of them. She began to comb out her red hair. 'And I really do look as good as my picture?' she badgered.

I nodded. I was smiling back even though I was feeling peeved inside that I had been forbidden to bring my sketchbook. I could at least have tried to draw Chloe. Of course Tawney could have shown her standing like that with just a few pencil strokes. I watched how she was throwing her weight forward on to her right foot. . . .

She threw down her comb.

'Do you really want me to take you round Amberley?'

'Mmmmmm!'

'All right. It's a dare. Might take you. There'll have to be a condition. . . .'

'What do you mean?'

With a toss of her head she flicked her hair forward so that she was peering at me through the strands – and she would not answer directly.

'Never you mind. Got to think about that. Have to get my things on first. You sit over *there*. And talk to me while I'm doing it – go on.'

So I sat a little awkwardly and looked away out across the river. The cart-horse seemed to have settled down again.

Chloe simply stood where she was in the marigolds and continued drying.

'You're not talking,' she complained.

'What do you want me to talk about?'

'You have to choose that – otherwise you're not doing the talking.'

I supposed she was right. I noticed out of the corner of my eye that she had half wriggled out of the black swimsuit – and here was me without even a sketch-book. I saw how her freckles trickled right down her back.

'You're still not saying very much,' she said over her shoulder.

'Chloe?' I asked in a rush.

'Yes.'

'Will you take me round Amberley church?'

'The church? Ooh – there is something I'd like to show you in there.' Her voice was coming through her jersey now. She was finding it quite a business steering all that hair through the neck.

'So – so you will take me then?' I asked the waving green jersey.

Chloe's eyes emerged.

'Probably. Only there is the condition. You . . . you might not want to do . . . what I am going to ask you.'

'What *is* the condition then?'

'Matt, will you come to the weir with me?'

I could not see her face. For a moment I was able to see where round her stern she had no freckles at all. I went back to looking across the river.

'Isn't the weir – up in the Amberley Mounds?' I asked.

'Mmmm! Have to go up there, sometimes. It's very lonely – when you get that far.'

Somehow, Chloe being lonely, Chloe being really lonely, had not struck me before. I looked back at her. (All at once I was imagining her being not quite so confident, but me there as well, as a sort of compensation.)

48

'I'll come with you – if Tawney lets me.'

'He'll let you. If I ask him he'll let you.'

I supposed Tawney would. I supposed Tawney would laugh at me. It wasn't going to matter if he did. I watched Chloe finish dressing and fold up her wet swimsuit in her towel.

'C'mon,' she said. 'Like me to carry your pyjama jacket with my things?'

I decided that I would carry my own jacket.

We did not go straight back across the Green to Amberley. Chloe preferred to lead me another way round, by the edge, under a long line of willows. It was like slipping into the village by the back door. We came round the end of a hedgerow and all at once I could again see the church tower standing up like a stubby thumb over the thatched roofs. She did not say a word to me until we got to this point.

'See that other grey stone tower thing – nearer to us than the church – that used to be the village lock-up. Not that anyone can remember anybody ever being locked up in it. We used to muck about in there when I went to school. Supposed to be the only bit left from an old priory. Monks all died in a plague. An archaeologist dug up the field round there and found a whole lot of graves. That was a few years back. The old boy who did the digging's dead now.'

She had paused – was hesitating – almost as if she did not want to go in the village at all.

'You don't go to school here now?' I asked.

'Can't anymore,' Chloe said shortly.

She walked ahead quickly, up on to the village street. I followed, imagining she must now go to some school in the county town maybe. When she actually stepped on to the road, she paused again, looked left and right, and waited. It was a narrow little street that twisted round between the closely built cottages.

'This way?' I asked. I could not see that there was any other direction.

'Y-e-s. You are going to keep with me, aren't you?'

'I want to,' I told her.

Chloe took a deep breath. For an instant she stood there, just looking, seeming almost more curious than I was. She bit her lip, hesitated, I almost thought she was going to turn away, and then she reached down for my hand and we did go forward. And yet, it was as if there were weights on her feet, we went so slowly.

We went, over the cobble-stones, between the two lines of staring cottage windows that seemed all lace curtains and flower boxes. We stopped and stared at a canary in a brightly painted cage sunning itself above us on the rough flint wall. We looked at a cottage where the ivy had grown so tight around it that the tiny windows could hardly see the street at all. We passed an old woman crouched down on her knees and scrubbing her step already dazzling white. Chloe stopped and looked at everything.

'It's still all the same,' she said. She looked back. One could see the Green. Then she pointed forward. The street was bringing us out into a little square. We walked on into it.

Chloe stopped – stood – she was looking all round.

'Used to have the village pump here . . . and the stocks. They've all gone, but there's something else still here. Look Matt, up on the wall under there – high up – see it?'

I did see it, the second time. *It* was set in a little niche, almost under the eaves of one of the old houses. It was a little stone face, heavily worn and weathered, leaning forward and poking out its tongue.

'Who is it – or what is it?' I asked. I had to stand right back and up on my toes at the same time.

'D'you mean Tawney's never told you? That's the Amberley Brat. Nobody knows who ever did it or quite why they put it up there. But it fascinates Tawney and he sat here all

50

one afternoon once, on the top of a very tall ladder, drawing it. The constable got upset 'cause he said it blocked the traffic. Here! So Tawney had to finish at five the next morning. C'mon – this way round.'

'Well – give me a chance to look,' I complained. She was so impatient. The face . . . one could not make out if it was a boy or girl. But Chloe dragged me on.

We crossed over what was the main street, the one I had come down in the coach. I spotted the village shop. There was a bunch of village ladies all gossiping outside.

'This way,' Chloe insisted, going straight over, avoiding the ladies.

'Do you know,' I said to her, 'that Tawney has told the shop they mustn't sell me anything today? Not a pencil, a ball-point, or anything – to make sure I won't draw!'

'Because he doesn't want you to draw?'

'I told you. He only wants me to look at everything.'

'Oh, Tawney can get our village to do anything – anything! They all think he's mad yet they all like him. He's awfully hard to say no to. Through the gap in the wall here!'

Unexpectedly . . . we were right over in the far corner of the churchyard. Chloe had paused. I was behind her. Her red hair swung left, right, as if to see who might be about, yet here there was nobody. I was seeing it for the first time in the light, seeing over the graves and between the trunks of the yew trees and up the paths that led to the grey stone walls. It was cool and peaceful here, the sunlight dotting through the branches and down on to the tombstones. Some of them were overgrown, were covered in moss and ferns, some fallen. Others, even some of the old ones, were well tended, had become sudden little gardens. We stood, side by side on the path by an old seat. Someone had dropped some marigolds. I gazed at a stone: 'Sacred to the memory of Maria Buckett, died 1888.'

'Gargoyles,' Chloe was saying, pointing up at the church roof.

I had seen pictures of them, had heard about them from my father . . . they were supposed to be unusual for they all had huge beards. They were carvings of old men's heads and waists leaning far out from the edge of the church roof, and were really there to shoot the rain water clear of the stone walls. I stared up. The gargoyles all had their hands clasped behind their heads and half of them were smiling and the other half just scowled.

'But it's in the church you've got to see – what I want to show you – what Tawney'll ask you all about. C'mon!'

I had wanted to stop and have a proper stare at those gargoyles – but she had got hold of my hand again. I had to follow.

With an easy familiarity Chloe swung back the wire-netted outer door to the porch. (She told me it was to keep out the birds.) Then she closed it carefully behind us before turning the massive black iron handle of the proper door. I can remember standing there, looking at the usual church notices: the appeal for the cathedral funds, the Amberley Midnight Fête and Fair, the lists of the bell ringers. There was a place in the ancient wall that must once have held holy water. I saw that a marigold had been pushed in.

'Here we are,' Chloe half whispered to me. The main door creaked.

It struck me as cold inside. I wondered how cold it must seem to Chloe with her bare feet on the stone flags though she did not appear to notice. It was dim here – one could see the stained glass windows full of blues and browns, a single beam of sunlight from a side chapel, the long and empty oaken pews. My sandals clanked over a grating.

'Over here,' Chloe whispered. 'It's right at the back. Tawney made it. I like to think it's the best thing in the church.'

I followed her, wondering what it was going to be.

It was set in a hollow in the thickness of the old wall – carved in stone, a not very long stone box. Carved along its

52

side in a high relief . . . was a water rat running through rushes.

I opened my mouth – and then shut it again.

Piled beneath it, covering both the inscription and the date, was a mass of marigolds.

It was as if Tawney had brought the dead stone to life and had started it running. His water rat had a wonderful tail and feet, his rushes were growing.

'It's Tawney who is really marvellous,' Chloe whispered in my ear.

Yet it was at this exact moment that I came to realise that Chloe and I were not alone in the church. Sitting to one side and staring at us . . . and now rising to her feet, was the middle-aged woman with the streaky iron-grey hair. It was from my face that Chloe realised that someone else was here . . . and looked round.

The woman herself was smiling at me in recognition, was coming forward to speak – while Chloe looked from the woman to me and back again, as if something had gone wrong, as if she could not think what we were going to say. Chloe looked as if she had been suddenly caught out, as if we were doing something wrong.

'Hello,' Chloe broke in quickly, and in her full voice, not in a whisper at all, so that she made me jump.

Yet the woman took no notice of this, no notice at all. She took no notice of Chloe springing up towards her, but only of me.

'Hello Matt – you have found your way here then. D'you know what you're looking at? D'you know who did it? It's nothing less than your friend Tawney's masterpiece. I think it is. *He* won't have any of it, mind you – about the work being any good. He will ask you all about the font carvings and the Tudor pulpit and those brasses over there.'

'It's not his masterpiece,' Chloe burst out. 'It is good but it's not his masterpiece. It isn't even his sort of thing. You know it isn't. I know why you think it's a masterpiece.'

53

The woman jerked her head, pulling her face away from where Chloe stood, her taut smile now vanished. I realised that she must be in some sort of pain. But it was as if the woman's own looking away was what hurt – not the looking at Chloe. Yet she made herself look only at me, although I was of no importance.

'I'll take myself off and leave you to look round the church by yourself, in peace. I know Tawney will want you to have a good look at it. See you later on, Matt.'

She walked, rather quickly, down the aisle.

I stood there, just feeling terribly embarrassed. But Chloe ran round ahead of her, got to the big door first, unlatched it and pulled it open for her, held it so wide open that a flood of sunlight came pouring into the building.

The woman seemed nonplussed by this, seemed uncertain what to do – whether to walk out into the porch ... or for some reason, to leave by a completely different door. And yet Chloe was holding the door open for her. They were hardly a yard from each other. Then I saw Chloe reach out a hand and just touch her sleeve.

'Good-bye,' Chloe said, unexpectedly, and yet although that was what she said she did not seem to mean good-bye. It was rather as if she was pleading for something, as if the woman would know just what she was pleading for. The woman swayed, as if Chloe's touch had been some sort of blow, and then without a word she brushed past Chloe and went out into the porch. For an instant I saw Chloe watch her go, watch the woman open the outer door of netting beyond, fumble with the catch, open it and shut it sharply behind her. Then, and suddenly I was thankful, Chloe swung her heavy door shut again and once more we were alone in the half light of Amberley church.

'Do you know who that was, Chloe?'

Chloe was pale, almost as if she was unwell. She nodded.

'Oh yes,' she said slowly. 'I know who that is. I've – I've

always known her. She . . . but hasn't Tawney told you? No – he can't have told you then.'

Chloe stopped. She was looking over my shoulder at the tomb that Tawney had carved for the church. For a moment I was afraid that she was going to cry. She pushed back the red hair from her face. I found myself so wanting to say something that might help and finding that I had no idea what to say.

'She – she never forgets the marigolds,' Chloe went on, 'even after all this time. I'm sorry this had to happen now. It was being a lovely morning. Let me – let me show you all the other things. Don't think I want to look at this just now.'

So we didn't look at it anymore.

'You'd better go back to Tawney now,' Chloe said. 'It will be time for his snack. I know. It always is. I'd better leave you here. We might go up to the weir tomorrow. I'll try and see you first thing. You will try and come – won't you?'

'I'll come, Chloe,' I promised. I wasn't quite sure how. I followed her out of the church. It seemed that there wasn't anything else that she thought I ought to see. I would have liked to have gone round more slowly, I would have liked to have gone back to Tawney's own carving, but I did not insist. Chloe closed the main door behind us, pushed me out into the sunshine and then she closed the outer door.

'You won't tell Tawney too much, will you?' she asked me softly. 'Not this time.' And then, while I was wondering what I was not supposed to be telling Tawney, Chloe leaned over and kissed me.

'Don't you want to kiss me back?' she was asking.

I supposed that really I did. I stopped asking myself so many questions and just sort of kissed her back. She was awfully warm and then she laughed and with a wriggle she was out of my arms – and running full pelt down the church-yard path.

For a moment I stood still, not certain if I should follow her. And then, I saw the Rector, awkward on his bicycle, coming through the gateway . . . and it was obvious that he saw Chloe running towards him, because he swerved, Chloe swerved, the Rector wobbled madly.

'Eeeeeh!' the Rector screamed, both loudly and somewhat unexpectedly. But he hadn't yet fallen off! He seemed to sway on that bicycle for what seemed like forever and then there he was tumbling off and sprawling down among the gravestones. I found myself running towards him. It was only when I reached the Rector that I realised that Chloe wasn't anywhere.

The Rector was getting on to his feet, a little shakily, and was rather ruefully dusting down his suit. I picked up his bicycle.

'Thank . . . thank you, Matt.' It was a controlled voice. 'A bit unintended I am afraid. My imagination runs away with me sometimes. I suppose I wasn't looking where I was going. No – I am all right, I think. Just got back from Tawney actually, left him getting your lunch. No – no, I will take the bike. . . .'

He hobbled away.

5

'You've had a good morning,' Tawney told me through his kitchen window, and . . . 'it's all laid out in the garden,' he shouted, having disappeared from sight. 'What are you carrying your pyjamas for?'

But he had gone so I did not have to answer.

It was not altogether my idea of a garden. It was really a sort of clearing where the grass had been trimmed down and the undergrowth hacked back from around a weeping tree. But there was a trestle table under it and benches – one down either side – while the table itself had been well and truly laid! I counted five sorts of cheese on a board – not to mention a cream cheese with herbs in an earthenware bowl. There were three kinds of bread too, and baskets of greengages and pears, while in the centre – a mountain of green grapes. Sunlight spotted through the leaves and dappled all the table-top. Under the tree it was like a tent and I was left wondering if I was supposed to sit down, or to go back and offer to help, or what.

Then Tawney appeared behind me with a jug of cider and two mugs and told me where to sit – but he had forgotten the butter so I went and fetched it from his little scrubbed kitchen.

'Your dad always likes this stuff,' he said, indicating the cider. 'Well – go on boy – taste it!'

I remember it was a bit dry.

'You like it boy, don't you? Of course you do. But never too much! Terribly bad for the liver, boy. I know – my liver's terrible. Hope you managed to do something this morning. Tell you what I did – a whole lot of nothing! Reverend Benn! He was here the whole morning. Marvellous! Great friend of mine. Always beg and pray I won't see him while I'm working. But it was no good today. His prayers were bigger than mine. Always do talk when Benn comes. Enjoyed myself, worse luck! Bread?'

I had bread. It was not very difficult to imagine Tawney talking. I watched the way he was waving his arms about now. I wondered how the Rector talked back.

'It must have been him who passed me going,' I suggested.

'It was. He mentioned he had seen you.'

I thought I had better do some mentioning too.

'Saw him again on my way back – in the churchyard. He – he was falling off his bicycle.'

Tawney stopped sawing at the bread.

'Falling off? That's not like Benn. Was he all right?'

'Oh, I think so. I did pick his bike up for him. That's how I know.'

The bread knife went back into action.

'Good for you. Help yourself to that butter. See boy, I expect you think old Benn's just the usual sort of dear old rector. Don't you believe what you see. The Rector of Amberley's as hard as nails under that dog-collar. Seven years in the jungle he's been. Rumour has it that he was a cannibal witch-doctor! So you did get to the churchyard then? Where else did you get to? Let me ask you my big test question. If you've been a failure you may as well know right from the start. Where can you see the Amberley Brat?'

I did an imaginary jig all round Chloe. I could not get my answer out fast enough. Afterwards, I swore, I would thank her 200 times. I struggled to finish my huge mouthful of cheese.

'Isn't that what you see – it's a stone face high up on the wall – just round the corner from where the stocks used to be?'

'Bully for you!'

I watched Tawney being most satisfactorily impressed.

'Ha! And who told you about our stocks? Wasn't me. Must have been that rascal Benn. But did he have time? Not to fall off his bicycle *and* to tell you about the Amberley Brat surely? Perhaps you met Hester? Grey-haired woman talking about dancing on the Green? Yes?'

I had cut off a bit of Dutch cheese. My father always calls it soapy stuff, especially when I'm eating it. I like it. I like it even more when nobody is telling me how soapy it is.

'I did meet someone like that. She didn't tell me who she was – though she knew you all right – seemed to know who I was too. And she said that she had found this barn for you.'

I watched him listening to my reply, the dappled light all over him, his own face thoughtful and a little faraway.

'That would have been Hester,' he said softly. 'Owe you an explanation really. Never told you before – but now you are down here – you'll have to know.'

He picked himself off what must have been half the bunch of grapes.

'Hester and I,' he began very slowly and deliberately, almost as if he was rehearsing to himself, rather than talking to me. 'We are married, though we've been separated for some time. She . . . she won't come to the studio much these days, unless I'm unwell or something.'

Tawney looked up, seemed to have to look round to find me, seemed to want to see what I thought, rushed on before I could say anything.

'In fact I miss Hester more than I want to admit but I'm stupid enought to refuse to go back to the old cottage, much as I should like to. Yet she still – I mean she made all this bread and there is a chocolate cake because she knows you are staying here and so got old Benn to bring it over.'

'Oh,' I said, 'I see.' I didn't see at all.

'Yet we – we don't live together anymore – even though we like each other more than either of us cares to say. Something happened – perhaps it was because of me that it did happen. And I didn't behave too well afterwards. A lot of it's been my fault. All a bit silly, if you want to know the truth of the matter.'

'Oh!' I said again, rather uselessly, trying to get this sorted out in my mind and wondering what to say. 'I'm sorry. But it wasn't . . . your wife . . . who told me about the Brat.'

Tawney was dipping his grapes in his cider before eating them. It washed them, I suppose, but it seemed an odd idea to me.

'Who was it then, boy?' he wanted to know.

'Chloe,' I said. 'It was Chloe who took me all through the village. She was the one who told me about the stocks – and the Amberley Brat.'

Somewhere up behind us a wood pigeon cooed and called. I looked up – I looked back towards Tawney. He was seated there with a big green grape about to be popped into his mouth. But it did not get there. He just sat, his elbows on the trestle table, and stared at me.

'Chloe?' he asked wonderingly. He seemed to be asking his garden more than me. 'Chloe? You say you saw *Chloe* this *morning*?'

'Why yes . . . by the . . . you see . . . last night . . . she asked me if I would try and meet her.'

Tawney took a long slow drink of cider. He stared at me across the rim of his mug. I wondered what was the matter. I was realising that I must have given her away and I was kicking myself. But Tawney's question, when it came, was not quite what I had expected.

'Tell me Matt – in the daylight – how did she look to you? Was she . . . how was she . . . well? . . . happy?'

'She was great fun,' I told him. I heard myself say it.

60

Then an idea came into my head and I forgot to think before I spoke. 'D'you know that when I saw her she was just like your picture? She was even wearing the same swimsuit.'

It just slipped out. It took me two whole seconds to realise that it had come out.

Still he stared at me. Still he did not eat his grape. He did not even seem to have noticed the river bit.

'Did you . . . like her?' he asked me.

I nodded. I did like her but why did he ask like that?

'And I like her too, boy. Did she . . . did she ask you . . . did she ask you to swim?'

'Why yes, she did.'

The grape was put down. He turned his face away from me. He would not look me in the face.

'Er – I didn't go in,' I said lamely.

He groaned, and in a way it really frightened me. I had never heard a man groan seriously before.

'I am the idiot,' he said. 'Don't think I mind you swimming. And Chloe herself is a marvellous swimmer. But you see, you told me about her last night and I did not even have the sense to warn you. I said nothing. I'm thankful you're still all right. For you must not swim with Chloe. Any of the other village girls – but not Chloe. No – you could not possibly have realised why – or understood. I hoped – stupidly – that you would not have to.'

I still did not understand.

'Hester – Mrs. Tawney – she did warn me that the river might be dangerous,' I began.

'It's not so much the river, boy,' he said. 'The river is obvious. It's not the river – it's Chloe.'

He was looking at me and I can remember that it was torture for him to tell me, but I could see too that he had to tell me, just as I had to ask him.

'Chloe? What is the matter with Chloe?'

'The matter? The matter is I have known old Chloe for a

very long time. Perhaps it is far too long. Matt . . . she is different . . . and I have to try and explain that difference to you.'

A cabbage white butterfly flapped through the space above our table – over the loaves and the half empty cider jug and the fruit. Outside the shade of our tree the sun glared down. Everywhere I could hear the zizz of the insects. I could feel all the heat. My clothes stuck to me a little. I could not grasp what Tawney was really trying to say. I could only feel the deep anxiety with which he was trying to say it. I knew I was oddly sick.

'Go over to the studio for me, boy. My picture of Chloe is still left out on the chair. Bring it back and we will look at it out here.'

I found it easily enough. I was glad to be able to look at it, to stand there in the empty studio and look at it all by myself. It was marvellous how Tawney could paint her red hair as it flowed down her back. I could even see drops of water on the freckles of her shoulder. One of her shoulder straps had slipped. This was just how Chloe did stand. I could only stare at that canvas wishing that I too could make mere paints make her.

It seemed so normal, just staring at that picture. But Tawney wanted me to carry it outside – wanted me to make it normal no longer. Yet I did carry it out into his garden – carried it not wanting to take it, not wanting, suddenly, to know anything about it.

He managed to hang his picture on the tree. It was as if he had done this before. There was a nail. We both sat down again while he looked at his own work, looked at it so heavily as if he did not like it, and yet would have liked to have liked it. I thought he was never going to speak.

Very deliberately, he began to peel a pear.

62

'Have you looked at the date?' he asked.

I looked at him. Then I looked at the canvas. There was a date there, tiny in the bottom right-hand corner, tinier than his tiny signature, but very clear.

It was twenty-five years previously.

I stared at the face on the canvas, at Chloe looking back at me over her shoulder.

Twenty-five years ago!

'Then – then this can't be Chloe,' I stammered.

Chloe looked back at me from out of Tawney's canvas.

'I am afraid that this is Chloe,' Tawney said gently. 'We are sitting here together Matt, here in the sunshine, and we are looking at my portrait of Chloe. I painted this all of twenty-five full years ago. And you have seen her this morning. She has not grown up, has she? I have to tell you, I am sorry, but Chloe can never grow up . . . not now. She is always going to look . . . like this.'

I went on staring at the canvas, staring as if my eyes could fight through and come out on the other side. I had to stare and stare at the canvas and only at the canvas.

'Who – who is Chloe, please Tawney?'

'Our daughter, Matt. Hester's and mine.'

I knew that he had put a piece of pear into his mouth. I could hear his heavy jaws chumping up and down. I had to wait for that chumping to stop. My mind was bursting with what he had said, with what Chloe had not said, with a terrible bewilderment and a terrible understanding.

'But . . . she is well, isn't she?'

'Well – and not exactly well, Matt. You see, it was twenty-five years ago that Chloe went swimming above the Amberley weir, went swimming all by herself. We had let her go a bit wild, Matt. Our fault! Though she was a powerful little swimmer. Hester and I weren't agreeing very much at the time. It was our friend Benn who found Chloe's body after it had been washed over the weir. Single-handed he managed to get her out. Then, still alone, he carried her nearly two

63

miles to the nearest railway station – it was the only place – and the trains ran in those days. Little Oaken Station – even then it didn't do much more than serve a quarry. Hester and I – they put on a special engine from Amberley to get us there. I shall never forget that ride. It was dark by that time. There was the flare from the fire-box – we had to hang on to the swaying engine cab – they went as fast as they could. It would have been three times as far by road. The message was a bit garbled and we still hoped that she was alive. When we got there – they had put her in the waiting-room – on the table. It was a cold little room. There wasn't anything that either of us could do. Nobody blamed us. We both knew that we were both to blame. Oddly enough, that was something we never disagreed about. I remember standing there with Hester, looking at Chloe, hating myself and helpless. The others thought I was mad. You see, I started drawing Chloe, as she lay there. Drawing was all I knew, the only thing that came to me then. That was one thing Hester did understand, bless her. That drawing of Chloe's head I showed you last night, that was it. I did that twenty-five years ago.'

I seemed to hear his words without listening to them. Part of my mind refused to understand – another part understood only too well.

'But who have I been talking to?' My voice no longer sounded like my voice.

Tawney ate another piece of pear. He did not speak to me at all. He spoke to his own fingers.

'Chloe's ghost.'

Again I watched his jaws eat. And I knew that I believed him – even if I could not quite believe in my own belief.

'Before last night,' he was saying, 'Chloe really only came back to me, here. Oh, she tries to appear to Hester too – at our original cottage by the Rectory – but Hester refuses to see her. My wife is rather common-sense. She considers that seeing ghosts is a sort of weakness. I think she feels that the village would think her a bit dotty. The village does think that I'm a bit dotty, of course. But time after time Chloe does come back . . . and talks to me. Always she is as she has always been. She talks nineteen to the dozen as she always did, about everything and anything – except as to why she came back. Chloe only laughs when I ask her that. There are moments when I feel – almost that she is waiting for me to tell her why she has to come. She comes so often that I have long got used to her. Yet Hester still grieves terribly over our lost daughter . . . while in a curious way I have never lost her at all. If Chloe misses a few weeks then I am disappointed. But then she reappears again – she plays around the barn and chats to me – as she always has. I look forward to her coming. But so far – she has only visited me really. And now you, Matt, a comparative stranger, you have seen her in the full day, and last night when you arrived, then you saw her. Perhaps I have been a fool to talk to her about you and your visit. But I talk to her about everything I do. Last night – I saw no point in saying who she was. But now it is you who have seen her in the middle of the morning – and you never even knew her!'

'The – the Rector's seen her,' I said. 'That – that's why he fell off his bicycle!'

Tawney looked down at his fingers.

'Then she's showing herself to the whole village! D'you know, if she had still been alive, she would have been thirty-nine by now. Hester will hardly be able to bear this – to see other people seeing Chloe as she once was.'

'But Chloe is real,' I heard myself burst out. 'She – she splashed water at me. I – I've held her hand.'

A glimmer of a smile crossed Tawney's face.

'She is real, my boy. She is a very real ghost.'

'But she's even pinched my pyjama jacket. You see – she came and saw me again last night – while I was going to bed – and then ran off with it. Had to see her today to get it back. That's why I had it with me.'

'Can't help that, Matt. She's been pinching my brushes, pencils, books, ever since she went. We play table tennis. She's none the less real for being dead – she's more! Yet in all these years she has never changed – she never grows any older – she is a ghost.'

'But I've seen her swimming and she has come out and *dried*,' I insisted, somehow certain that a ghost could not be wet.

'She even eats, Matt. Almost absentmindedly, a year after she was drowned, I offered her one of her favourite chocolates. She ate it! It disappeared! Then I found her turning up when I was having supper by myself and I would give her some. She didn't only enjoy it – she would forget to wipe her mouth – she would be stained with raspberries. And yet, Matt . . . when we get to the winter, that's where it shows. I remember one of the first times I noticed . . . it had been snowing all day and it was still snowing. It was very late, and very cold . . . and all at once, in she came. She sat at my side, sat down on the rug, bare feet, bare legs, hair down her back. It had never struck me before – I put out my hand and felt her hair – it was sprinkled with snow. I tickled the back of her neck – Chloe always liked that. And then I realised that she was still wearing nothing under her jersey and that she ought to have been frozen. Yet she was still brown, she was six months dead and she still felt as if she had just been running in the sun, she was so warm.'

I remember Tawney sitting there at his trestle table, scratching the back of his head – and hardly talking to me, talking rather to himself. I thought of the old horse that morning, who had run away from Chloe, and now I knew why. All at once I was feeling . . . so very sad.

'Why – why do you think she keeps coming back?' I asked. Inside a part of me was also asking – Come back from what? – What keeps coming back?

'She doesn't tell me,' Tawney said flatly. 'She will not say anything about what happened, what happens, what she

66

wants to happen, now she is dead. She seems only to continue on and on as if she never slid over the weir that afternoon, as if it all never happened at all. She does know that it isn't still twenty-five years ago – but that's not something she ever wants to discuss.'

It was at this moment that I made a discovery about myself. I had promised to see Chloe again. Somehow I knew that I must not tell Tawney what I had promised. And then it followed from that . . . I realised it . . . I was in no way changing my mind. Mad as it was I was still going to see Chloe. A whole side of me was not running away.

I watched Tawney's hands feeling their way around the table for more grapes that were no longer there . . . they were disappointed. His cider jug was empty too. So he just went on talking . . . and his talking seemed so much more extraordinary than Chloe herself had ever been.

'And you see, boy – before she drowned – how I used to draw her. I was always drawing her – because she was always there. You've seen one or two things – but there are many, many more. Best model I ever had. She would put up with me for hours. Yet now she is dead she won't sit for me, she won't let me paint her. I made a few attempts at first, but she stopped me altogether. I have asked her over and over again. Now she even gets into a kind of temper if I as much as look at any of my old things of her. That is why I hid this picture away – because Chloe can't bear it! I have to hide them all away. I can only bring them out . . . when I feel that she's not here.'

He talked on and on. He kept on talking until I reminded him that he was supposed to be teaching me – just to stop him. So we did the washing up together and he sat me down in the barn and at last we began. But all the time I could see that his heart was not in what he was doing, and that I was hardly listening either. It was not like Tawney at all.

He made me hide Chloe's picture away.

I did see another one of her on the rack – she was eating an apple.

Tawney sent me out to draw. We were almost glad to escape from each other.

6

I did not go near the village. I did not go near the river. I did not go very far. I simply found and followed a small path that led me off the road and allowed me to be alone. It took me round the back of some old farm buildings and through a strong smell of pigs. Then it took me up the side of a field of turnips and through a hedge over a stile and then up again on to the open side of a hill. There was a stone wall there and there I sat and sat looking down at the view.

Again I could see the whole of Amberley, but the other way round and from further away, compared with the morning. Now I could see more of the Green and what must have been part of old Bascombe's house and the roof of Tawney's barn. This time I was seeing it alone.

I could see it and yet I could not quite believe in it. Yesterday, at this time, I had been sitting in the coach. Now I sat up here. This morning I had talked to Chloe and it had been a somehow strange and yet marvellous morning. This afternoon I had been with Tawney and that morning had become all bewildered. Now I was alone and Chloe had been made different. Tawney had at no time told me what to do and none of the things that I had seen or the things that he had told me would quite join up in my head. So I tried to sit still.

I tried to tell my mind to stop going over and over, to stop asking questions. I did try to make myself look round. Nobody seemed to be about. I got out my sketch-book, not certain that this was the right place to work – not just now.

Sunlight glinted on the distant river. I could see a line of long puffy white clouds sailing up from the south between the Mounds. A jay flapped over a tree.

At least I was allowed a pencil this time . . .

Well – I hadn't been forbidden one!

I opened to a blank page in the sketch-book. Then I looked in front of me, considered what I saw, and finally I put a small upright mark on the paper, dead in the centre. That was the church. It did not look like a church – but that was what it was. As soon as one makes a mark on an empty sheet of paper . . . then that sheet of paper has a place inside itself, an inner shape that it has never had before. You have begun and you can never go back on it.

I sat on my wall.

I looked up at the Mounds on either side. How was I going to parcel them all out? I looked down at my paper.

And then I was hearing footsteps – already! I did not look up. I refused to look up. I went on sitting and holding my pencil. My first thought was that I hoped whoever it was would not want to stop and talk. I had had enough of talking. I wanted Tawney's notice pinned to the back of his sweater: GO AWAY – CONFOUND YOU!

The footfalls seemed to come quickly up to me – and then stop. I knew that whoever it was was standing close to me, was looking over my shoulder. So I had to look round.

It was the middle-aged woman with the iron-grey hair. It was Hester Tawney. She was standing there – waiting for me to notice.

I put down my pencil.

'Hello . . . Mrs. Tawney.'

'Hello Matt.' She was smiling. She smiled with her eyes rather than her mouth. I could see all the countless little lines smiling at the corners of her eyes. 'So you know now? Yes – I am Mrs. Tawney. I even enjoy being Mrs. Tawney still. There . . . there are only a few things that we really disagree about, Tawney and I.'

I didn't know really, but I nodded and hoped that that was the right thing to do.

I was glad that she did not try and look at my sketch-book with its solitary mark. I certainly did not want to talk about that.

'It's his work,' she said shortly. 'My fault – I knew well enough what he was like before we ever got married. Everything always goes into his work. Anything else, anyone else, comes second. It was all right when I was his work. He used to paint me in those days. He was always painting me. I must have been the best model he has ever had. He sold everything he ever did of me. They were – our work. I liked being with him. He liked me being there. But I thought, when we got married, that we should have been able to do – just most things together. But with him his work was always just that bit more important. It was not that we didn't get on. He still thinks I'm marvellous. Likes me to be there. Always wants me to be with him . . . even if he doesn't say anything to me for hours and hours. But it is always his work that really has to come first.'

'Yes,' I said, listening to this outburst and wondering if it was half aimed at me. But Mrs. Tawney hardly seemed to be noticing me here at all.

'Then we had a daughter.'

'Chloe,' I prompted.

'So he has told you that?'

'Oh yes,' I said, all at once afraid of what she might say.

'He's told you . . .?'

'I've seen some of his pictures of Chloe,' I said.

'Yes – he would show you those.' She stopped. She started again. 'He has never sold any of them. He doesn't need to. I wouldn't want him to.'

'In the church,' I began a little awkwardly. I had to say something. 'Where you had put all the marigolds . . .'

'That's where Chloe lies,' Hester Tawney said.

A breeze blew across my face. I managed to shut my

sketch-book. I didn't want it open now. Somehow I still wasn't being allowed to draw. I had come to Amberley to draw – to learn to draw – and Tawney did want me to draw, but now I was becoming part of the Tawneys instead. *Chloe Tawney*, my mind said to me. I had not thought of that before.

'It was because of Chloe that you did not want me to swim,' I said.

Hester was looking out over the same distance that I had been looking over. She was looking away from me.

'That's right, Matt dear. Chloe was always swimming. It was as if she escaped from us all once she was in the water.'

There was a difficult pause.

'Matt – when I saw you – a little later this morning? When we were in the church? There was somebody else there, wasn't there? Apart from you and me? You were with someone, weren't you? I don't mean to be curious – but there was somebody there, wasn't there?'

I felt as if I had been caught in the wrong place with the wrong person. But surely Mrs. Tawney saw too? I was not sure what to say.

'I was with someone,' I admitted. 'I . . . I didn't understand why you did not speak to her. You – you must have known who I was with.'

Hester Tawney was looking at me directly now.

'All these years, Matt, I have been seeing that hallucination – ever since Chloe drowned. I have seen her – in my garden, bouncing a ball – or she has come in and put down her books from school at half past four. I have walked into my own bathroom and she has left all her usual mess after washing her hair! And I have tried so hard not to see her. Yet now even strangers see my hallucinations. The whole of Amberley would have thought I was going mad if I had talked about it. I thought I was going mad. A silly middle-aged woman's delusion! I have watched Chloe come up and speak to me. I have forced and forced myself not to make any reply. I have walked into her old room on a Sunday morning and then seen her asleep, years after she had died. I have made myself walk out again. I have gone in later and seen her bed unmade – and I have refused to remake it. I always used to insist that she made her bed. Besides – how could her bed be there unmade? Yet later I would find it made. So I had imagined it, hadn't I? Tawney kept telling me that he saw her. I blamed him for putting the whole idea into my head. I only wanted Chloe to be at peace. I didn't want her to keep coming back. Though I missed her – and I still miss her. I blame her too. Chloe was always so independent. She was a very good swimmer and she should have had more sense than to have swum out above the weir. But Tawney was always encouraging her to do things her own way. Perhaps that's why I haven't been able to forgive him. And when Chloe was found – d'you know the Rector found her? We had to go to Little Oaken Railway Station. That's where they laid her – on the table in the waiting-room. She was dead and Tawney hardly spoke to me. All he could do was just stand there and draw her!'

I could only sit on the stone wall, going both hot and cold at once and only knowing that I liked Tawney and that it was a tremendous drawing and that I liked Chloe too.

'And now you are seeing her, Matt. You are parading her even, up and down in front of her own mother. You must not see her. She is a madness and she is not real and she is not there!'

I opened my mouth and shut it again. Mrs. Tawney was almost shouting at me.

'Does she speak to you?'

'Why – yes, she speaks to me.'

'She never speaks to me. I won't listen to her. Why should she speak to you? Does – has she told you why she comes back? I don't understand why Tawney doesn't know. Why hasn't he told me?'

'He doesn't know,' I said. 'Chloe won't tell him.'

73

'He imagines her,' Hester declared. 'But he won't imagine why she comes back.'

'I don't think he imagines her,' I ventured.

She looked at me. There was a look of pain on her face. I could not make out what she really thought.

'If Chloe tells you, Matt – if Chloe tells you why she comes back – you will come and tell me, won't you?'

'Of course I will, Mrs. Tawney.'

All at once she turned very quickly – stopped – looked back at me.

'Thank you, Matt.'

And then she started walking away with jerky little steps back down the hill.

I just went on sitting, my hand stroking the familiar hard cover of my own sketch-book, over and over again. I sat there a long time. I felt terribly sorry for her. But I knew I was terribly sorry for Tawney too.

And for Chloe . . .

7

That night I at last got back to my room. I did not feel that I wanted to go to bed and yet I was so tired. It was long past the time when I ought to have gone to bed. Did Chloe have to sleep?

And I did not even know if Chloe could sleep. I only knew that I had to sleep. I had come up to this room to sleep.

Hadn't I already seen her in this room? The window was shut this time. The first thing I did on coming in was to see if it was shut. I remember looking out of that window and seeing . . . seeing nothing! It did occur to me that I had not seen a ladder anywhere – not one that would reach up this high.

This was the room where Chloe used to sleep when it was new. They were her mirrors that watched me getting ready for bed, that watched me look back at myself, that watched me put my comb through my hair, that saw me pulling off my shirt. Staring into her mirror over the dressing-table I could see her mirror over her basin, her full-length mirror on her wardrobe door. Like me, Chloe must have looked at the reflection of the white sloping walls of this plain high wooden room built in the roof of Tawney's barn. I stared at it in the mirror over the basin. I watched myself wash. I saw myself undress and fold up my clothes. Chloe's wardrobe door creaked, clicked, shut awkwardly. I could see a reflection of three of my reflections shutting three reflected wardrobe doors. How often must Chloe herself have padded round this room?

Chloe was not here.

The night was hot. I got straight into bed with only a sheet. Apart from Tawney himself I had not expected to meet anyone much on this holiday. My dad had never said anything to me about Tawney being married! And Tawney was supposed to be one of Dad's best friends. I had rather looked forward to coming down here and drawing with Tawney without being interrupted . . .

I was lying on my back. I kept lifting my head off the pillow in order to look all round the room. In the mirrors my reflected head came off the pillow and looked all round the room. None of Chloe's things were here. There were only my things. I could see my handkerchief, keys, knife, money, sandals on the floor.

This was Tawney's house! And today – today had been the first time I had ever seen Tawney at a loss. Before, he had always been the great man, the artist other people talked about, the big confident man who had only to ask and everything was opened up to him because he was . . . Tawney! My mother used to say that he was a good friend not just because he could make the day seem so much more interesting but he could make you feel more interesting as well. He would always want to listen to you. He had been a marvellous pal to me. But today I had seen him having to be uncertain, having to untie all his secrets in front of me and try to put up a good front, at a loss as to what he should do. But, didn't I like him all the more?

He was a giant-sized adult. Yet all at once I was having to share his life with him. Chloe was real. Hester was real. I could not understand what was happening but because I was involved with them all . . . because I liked them all, it made everything better and worse at the same time.

I was lying on my pillow and realising that I had not switched out the main light. I told myself that I would not switch it off just yet. Part of me was simply not sleepy. Would I be able to go to sleep? I could see the reflection of the light in the wardrobe mirror . . .

76

I sat up. Everything was quite still. I lay down again. I think I must have gone off to sleep with the bedroom light full on and my eyes wide open.

Everything felt so different in the morning. When I actually awoke it was to find myself very comfortable. For some reason I had never expected to be comfortable. I was opening my eyes and shutting my eyes and staring at the early sunlight on the sloping ceiling. A dog was barking somewhere in the far distance. I remembered watching Tawney, the night before, working on a painting of sunshine in his untidy garden. I had stood down there in the shadows of his studio, about to wish him a worried good night, and had remained there for ages, spellbound, seeing him create his own sunlight.

Now I was staring up at real sunshine . . . but there was the main bedroom light still on. I should have slipped out there and then and switched it off before Tawney came up with the tea to wake me. But then bed was so very comfortable. Perhaps I closed my eyes.

I can remember opening them. A tap was running. Tawney had come! Perhaps, in all this sunshine, he would not even notice the light left on. Stealthily . . . I turned my head on the pillow.

It was Chloe.

I was looking at her bending over the basin in the sun. It was such an ordinary thing to be doing. She was brushing her teeth and managing to send a spray of toothpaste up the mirror.

I watched her holding her red hair out of the basin with her left hand. The sun shone full on her bare back – I could see the curve of her spine with its knobbles, the movements of her shoulder blade as she was brushing. I remember that if anything alarmed me at all it was the conviction that I was the one who should not have been there. It was as if it was me invading her rather than the other way round. Did she even know that I was in the room?

I caught sight of her face reflected in the basin mirror. Chloe was wiping her mouth. Our eyes met. She knew.

'You're using my towel,' I exclaimed.

The face put out a tongue. It still had some toothpaste left round one end of its mouth . . .

'Wondered when you'd wake up,' Chloe said.

I was discovering that Chloe actually there, only left me afraid of what Chloe might think. I was terrified of making a complete fool of myself.

'Thanks for the loan of your toothpaste,' she was saying. 'Never seen this make before. The new peppermint goo – with grit!'

I thought I'd better sit up.

'How long have you been here?' I asked.

'S'my room,' she told me. It was not exactly an answer that said anything. She turned round. 'You've got to get up as well,' she added pointedly. 'It's a long way. Sooner we're ready, sooner we eat breakfast, sooner we're gone.'

And Chloe just went on standing there, combing out her red hair with my comb, waiting for me to move. I had no idea what to do. It seemed so much safer in bed. Out there she was in a different world. To get up and put one's feet on the fitted carpet beside her . . .

'But –' I began. It was as if I was afraid of her just because she was a girl.

'Tawney won't mind us getting breakfast now. I often cook here. He won't wake up yet, anyway. He went on too late last night. I'll leave him a note. After all – he's always leaving me notes.' She stopped in the middle of her combing. She was staring up over my head. 'Hey – the light's on!'

I wasn't going to tell her. I got out of bed to change the subject as much as anything. I wasn't going to tell her that I'd left that light on because I was afraid of her.

Chloe fried bacon and sausages and tomatoes while I had to cut bread, watch toast and make tea. Chloe buzzed round preparing a big picnic at the same time so that there was no doubt we were going a long way. I had to concentrate hard not to look inefficient – she was so deft and bossed me in loud whispers. We were supposed to be doing everything ever so quietly so as not to wake Tawney, but I could not see that you could fry quietly. Chloe certainly couldn't. ('Now cut those sandwiches down the middle for me. No, use that knife, the clean one. And then you can wrap them up in the plastic foil. Here, let me do it!') I felt better sitting down and eating breakfast. I knew what to do there.

Chloe stuffed down an enormous breakfast. I had to make more toast.

And we had to wash up afterwards. I had to volunteer to wash because she knew where everything went. We left a big note propped up against Tawney's cornflake box – MATT AND ME OUT ALL DAY, LOVE CHLOE. I carried the picnic.

There was a hole in the hedge at the back of Tawney's garden. We went through that. The path beyond both led away from the road and in the opposite direction to Amberley. I had no idea of the way . . . all this was unfamiliar.

'You do still want to come with me, Matt?'

I had felt all right while we had been having breakfast. Eating breakfast was familiar.

'Of course I want to come.'

Chloe did not seem to be half so troubled by the brambles and nettles as I was . . . and yet her feet were bare.

'Matt?'

'Mmmmmm?'

'Now that you've stayed with him a bit – what d'you think of my dad?'

The path was narrow and overgrown here. I was concentrating on following her heels. She had freckles right down to her heels. It took me a moment to grasp the importance of what she was asking. Did she know then . . . that I knew? Surely she must realise that I now knew who she was. But did she? I had no way of being sure.

'Tawney . . .?'

She made no query.

'Tawney is even more Tawney than I ever thought he could be. His studio's just his world. He makes everything he sees and does belong to him. But you have to like it because he makes all the things you know seem bigger and better.'

I could not see her face because she was walking in front of me. But it brought it home – it really was her father we were discussing.

'That's just how he is, Matt. That's always been him. Have you noticed? Everybody calls him Tawney! Even I call him Tawney. D'you know his Christian name? You don't, do you? It's Fred! Fred Tawney . . . but nobody ever calls him Fred. Never heard anyone do that, not even Mum. He's just Tawney. There isn't any other.'

It was as if she so wanted to call her father Fred. Or so wanted somebody to call him that. She did not look back at me over her shoulder and I did not know what to answer. The path in front of us was coming out into a field. It seemed to give her a chance to change the subject.

'Race you across!'

She was running almost before I realised. And I was the one carrying the basket. I pounded after her and I can remember thinking how she was really a bit younger than me – even if she had been born so much earlier. I sprinted – I nearly caught up with her.

I think that was the moment when we both started laughing. She dodged sideways – I nearly stumbled – she doubled back – I followed. And then she was off at an angle and up a green bank. I swerved round after her . . . I could hear a touch of hysteria in my own laughter.

Ahead of me, high on the bank, Chloe was standing still. She had turned round and was waiting for me. She did not try to run. She was smiling. I found that I had been led up on to an old disused railway.

She stood so still.

There was no railway fence here. The track had once led above the level of the field – that was why there was a grass bank. The original lines had all been taken away and now there was only a simple path of cinders.

'Is this the disused Amberley line?' I asked.

Chloe first looked up and down the track. It was empty.

'I use it,' she said. 'This is the way I always come. It's mine. Even when the old trains ran – weren't many – there weren't ever other people up here. Now most of the village have forgotten that there ever was a railway. There's nobody now, 'cept me.'

Not that there was much actually to see. Just an embankment with old cinders on the top. I could smell the scent of dry grass. A cuckoo was calling above us in the trees beyond. But Chloe's voice was the only other human voice. It was curiously private . . . standing there.

I too looked up and down the track. I had to admit to the fascination of it. It was like stepping up and over on to a very other place. This cinder track was sweeping in from some elsewhere, was going round towards a distant cutting, running on towards some different destination.

'Where does it come from – go to?' I asked.

I could see why I liked it. Yet it was a disturbing liking. Her railway skimmed just above the fields – it was as if the hill before us opened a little to let us through. Her railway seemed to be in the countryside, to belong to it . . . and yet to be of something else.

'It's supposed to come up from Spilcombe Junction and

then through Amberley to here – then there's Little Oaken, Undermore, Swinbridge and down to the other main line at Watermouth – if you look at a map.'

The names did not mean too much to me.

'Which way do we go now?'

'Towards the cutting. Away from the village. This way.'

'And it'll take us up to your weir?'

'Oh . . . almost. Be your weir too. But there's lots of time before we need go there.'

There was sufficient room for the two of us to walk along the track together though Chloe walked rather to the side to avoid the cinders. There was no sign of the old rails. I did see a battered sleeper abandoned in the undergrowth, and later a mysterious sign, close to the ground, which just had '14' on it. Chloe took hold of my hand.

'Fourteen miles from the junction,' she explained. 'That's behind us. And we must be five miles from any place else.'

I could not think up a good reason as to why I should not hold Chloe's hand.

We were entering the cutting. It was like being within high walls. You looked up and there were the trees climbing above you on either side – you looked ahead and the cutting curved so that you could not see where it was leading. A dark bevy of rooks called back and forth above us, black wings and harsh echoes. We were taken out of the sunshine into cool shadow and then carried back into the glare again. There, up on the bank ahead, I could see it, half hidden by undergrowth and overshadowed by trees, we were being watched by a distant signal-box.

I was wishing that the railway was not quite so private. The cutting had closed round behind us. One could no longer look back at the open fields. Here, there was only Chloe and me. Chloe had hold of my hand.

I looked away.

'S'pose it's because you live in London,' Chloe was saying. Even her voice seemed out of place here. There was an oppressive feeling that one ought to whisper. And what was she talking about?

'I mean – you're not very brown, are you?' Chloe said.

'You only freckle,' I retorted.

It made her let go of my hand.

'Don't – don't you like my freckles?'

'I like *your* freckles,' I assured her. I did.

'I used to hate them – until one day I thought I might as well like them 'cause they're what I've got. People will tease you about them and they're all over me. Have you seen the big ones?'

She stopped and pulled up her jersey and I had to stop and inspect a lot of midriff. I could see her breathing.

'And they're so big and yet they never join up. And it's not your fault you not being brown if you live in London. D'you know I never ever went to London? They were always going to take me but never got round to it. Never will now.'

I answered without thinking.

'You should have come up and stayed with us, Chloe. We've got a spare room. You can even see the dome of St. Paul's from the window – if you stand on the end of the bed.'

Impossibly – I was picturing myself showing her round my own room with my posters and the magazine cuttings pinned all around the walls. I was imagining everything being ordinary and us all going through the drawings in my portfolio and drinking coffee out of the big brown mugs we had at home . . .

'Like to have gone to London,' Chloe said wistfully. She pointed up at the signal-box.

'Used to go up there, now and then. One of the signalmen was a friend of Tawney's. Used to invite me up into the box sometimes and I'd share his tea. Always had apple jam. Let me work the signals too – against railway regulations. Had to sit down whenever a train went by, so that nobody would see me.'

Now that we were coming up to the signal-box I could see that all the glass had long since fallen out of the big windows. The old wooden steps up the side were green and spotted with mould, some of the treads were actually missing and a bramble grew up through it all.

'Tell you – there's an old tap at the back that still works,' Chloe said. 'Show you and we can have a drink of water.'

The basket was dumped down. There was a narrow path through the brambles at the side. I edged round after her. The path was well trodden down but led simply to an old brass tap.

'I'm the only one that uses it now,' she said.

Chloe had to use both hands to make it turn. When the tap did move no water came at all for a moment . . . and then spurted so hard that she stepped back and trod on me. The tap gushed everywhere and she had to struggle to control it. I wished that there was more space on the path. It was hot, even hotter here, the insects buzzing in our ears, everything smelling of damp and rust and decay. I watched her crouch down and push back her hair, the face half turned up, the mouth drinking.

Why did she want to drink? Did she really drink? Why did she want me to come with her?

'Now you, Matt.'

Her feet were wet, she had soaked her skirt, she was wiping her mouth with the back of her hand.

I knew I was shaking my head. All at once – and I knew there was no logic in it – I knew that I could not drink there – I did not want to drink where she had been.

'No – no thanks.'

84

'But you're hot, Matt. It – it's the only drinking place I have. I know we've got some drink in the basket, but . . .'

'I'm just not thirsty,' I lied. I was certain that she knew that I was lying.

We backed out on to the track. Without a word I picked up the basket. We began to walk on through the cutting. I walked on one side of the cinders, she walked on the other.

'Matt?'

'Yes?'

'You – you don't like me now, do you?'

The cutting was even steeper and higher at this point, we were out of the sun, even the trees were disappearing.

Chloe came across the cinders. She hobbled on them a little and then she grabbed on to my hand. I wanted to throw her hand away. She would not let me. And her hand was as warm as mine and it could not be warm. It was an imitation of warmth.

'Tell me what's the matter, Matt.'

I could not. I was not sure. I was not sure about myself, about her, about anything.

'You're afraid, aren't you Matt?'

She spoke so softly. I told myself that if I did not look at her she was not there.

'I can't blame you. I think you're being awfully good. I've so often been afraid of what's happened to me – over and over again – and now there can't even be any running away – I have to stay with what's happened.'

'What do you mean? Why should I be afraid?' I snapped out at her and then knew that I was even more afraid of her actually answering, of her telling me herself.

She stopped on the path.

'Would you rather we turned back, Matt? We could have the picnic in a field off the track. We don't have to go on. We can plan a different sort of day.'

I had not expected that answer.

85

'Of course we're not going back,' I insisted. It was me gripping her hand now, forcing us on. Perhaps it was me finding out that I too, could not run away. It would have meant admitting that there was something to be frightened of, admitting it to myself. 'We've come this far, haven't we?'

'But you may not like it, Matt.' Chloe's voice wailed a little. She stood feet apart – jibbing. 'I'm sorry, Matt. I seem to be doing everything all wrong!'

Yet still I pulled her on. Chloe walked, awkward beside me and with a sort of glad stubborn unwillingness – and neither of us spoke. The cutting had begun to close right in, it had deepened further, it was going downhill. It had become black rock on either side with only mean fern and grasses clinging to the ledges. There was only just room for our track between the cliffs. Chloe dragged her feet. I dragged my feet. Once Chloe stopped altogether and pushed back against me.

'Are you sure you want to go on, Matt?'

We went on.

We rounded another slow and overshadowed curve. I can remember where a signal, the semaphore at stop and facing the other way, hung gaunt above our heads. At one place the rock had been hollowed out a bit beside the track.

'That's for the plate-layers,' Chloe said. 'So they can stand out of the way of a train.'

I grunted.

Chloe kicked at the dust.

'Doesn't this line ever get clear of this cutting?' I asked her.

Chloe did not reply. We walked on.

'Of course it comes out,' she said at last.

I did not reply.

'You would come,' she said, as if it was all my fault.

86

'But you must know how much further,' I said irritably.
'Yes, I do.'

The sides of the cutting seemed to be leaning in. I had the distinct feeling that the next curve was going to plunge us round into a black tunnel.

8

But in fact . . . the cutting fell away.

I pulled up short when I saw that. I even let go of Chloe. She stood away from me, just watching. She had been quite right. I did not want to go on. Yet not for any of the reasons I had expected.

. . . there, not 300 yards ahead, our track was leading out over a sunlit, sparkling, flowery, open meadowland. Somewhere a lark was singing, singing and spiralling down towards us. The air seemed fresher, emptier . . .

It was as if Chloe was waiting for me to make up my mind.

Out here, here on the other side of the hill, the land was not farmed and yet it hardly seemed to be wild. Perhaps it was used by sheep, though I could not see any. There were flowers everywhere – yet they seemed so small. We had come out into a new place.

But somehow it could only make me more afraid.

I could still see where the rail track went on, where it bent away, running up the valley, up towards distant trees and a high cliff gouged out of the further slopes. The whole meadow was a cloth of colours, of countless greens and pinks and yellows, with deliberate red outcrops of rock and shale spilling out among the flowers.

I tried to look away from Chloe.

The track might have led up through a careful garden. The whole meadow looked kept and cared for and yet so endlessly empty. There was this extraordinary sense that there could be no one here but our two selves. Everywhere the meadow bloomed in a somehow marvellous fashion yet this only gave me an uneasy certainty that I was simply trespassing. It was as if Chloe ought never to have brought me. It was if I should not be seen in this place with Chloe . . . and yet there was no one here to see us.

'Will you still come with me?' I heard Chloe ask.

I looked down. I could avoid seeing her by looking down. But even then I had to look at countless tiny blue flowers, at a silver butterfly skimming above their heads. I did not reply.

Chloe moved nearer. I could just see her feet.

'Look behind you, Matt.' She was pointing back the way we had come. I had to look.

It was towards the cutting. I knew my way back from there – yet now I could no longer see where we had come from. But what Chloe pointed to was a battered board by the track, reading in the other direction.

'WHISTLE', it said.

And as I looked at it, Chloe whistled!

I jumped from where I stood.

Chloe's whistle was a long riveting piercing warbling scream! She let go more shriek than whistle.

'When I was small,' Chloe said behind me, 'we used to go on the train along here. Sometimes I imagine it coming along here still. It was only a little train – on the one track. Whenever I walk along here, especially when it's dark, I think I can hear it steaming up behind me through the cutting. It used to really struggle up the gradient back there.'

For a moment I had to picture it too, the clouds of smoke and steam, the glow from the fire-box . . . yet I had to ask a question: 'How many years is it since they closed the railway?'

Chloe turned her face away at that – I knew that I should not have asked it, I knew that it was unfair to have asked her. Yet she smiled at me afterwards, though she did not answer.

For an instant I was staring at the sun on her hair and then she had spun an exuberant cartwheel away from me so that she would not have to answer. I could only watch her legs swing over, watch her come up on her feet as easily as she had gone down on her hands, and then she was running away over into her different world, over the green sward and the blue flowers towards the high overhanging trees. My mouth and nose were filled with the sweet clinging scent of honeysuckle. Chloe was looking back at me, feet apart, hair comically across her face. I knew I could only follow.

I told myself and told myself that I knew that she liked well fried tomatoes, that her father's name was Fred, that she wore pants that had blue polka dots on. These were ordinary things. I was even glad when she took hold of my hand because I was becoming afraid of myself. I had found myself wanting to run away from her and towards her at one and the same time.

The track at last leaned round to the right – unexpectedly – after we seemed to have been walking endlessly over meadows, and there, all at once, nestling under tall and gently waving trees, very alone and secret, was a railway station.

I did not have to be told where I was.

'Little Oaken,' Chloe confirmed. 'Nothing here now. Not really a place at all. Used to be a village and a quarry. When they closed the quarry the village went too.'

'Is – is that why they closed the line?'

'Didn't help. There was an awful row at the time. My mum was one of the protesters, not that we ever lived here. I remember her organising a meeting in Dad's studio, much to his surprise. And everybody ended up shouting.'

In spite of the fact that the railway lines had vanished it was so obviously a railway station. There was this huge sense of arriving in spite of the empty and overgrown appearance. Here was another signal gantry, this time without its signal, and there a porter's trolley without one wheel, lying where it had been left on a weed-covered heap of ballast. I found myself almost tiptoeing up the platform ramp where the grass and moss and dandelions now grew up between the stones.

Chloe had let me go on ahead.

Under the overhanging platform canopy were only blind and empty windows. I stopped to read the name-board, a bit missing, rather rickety: ITTLE O KE . The doors, unlike the windows, had originally been nailed up and now the nailing up had mostly fallen down. There were doorways for LUGGAGE, GENTLEMEN, WAITING-ROOM and a WAY OUT that led into a nettle bed. A smaller sign still asked one to SHEW YOUR TICKETS PLEASE. I wondered why they spelt it 'shew'. There was a shattered oil-lamp on a window-sill.

'If you're thinking of going in that Gents,' Chloe called out to me, '– don't!'

'Why's that?' I asked, somewhat absently.

'Floor gives way. You'd fall through. S'all rotten in there.'

'How do you know?'

' 'Cos I almost broke a leg. Would have been awful. There's almost no one ever about. Tawney won't ever come here now. Don't think he would even think of looking for me at this place – 'specially in there. Teach me to be curious. 'Course they haven't even *got* a Ladies.'

I stopped to look at the waiting-room. It was long and narrow, dank and in shadow. Water had got in at the other end and had stained the wall. There was a fungus growing over what must once have been a poster and the colours had streaked, faded and now bubbled. The floor was thick with dirt and leaves. Yet, in the centre, splattered with the droppings of birds, in this otherwise empty room, there was still the waiting-room table.

'Chloe,' I said.

There wasn't any reply.

When I turned round I saw, by itself, in the middle of the platform, our picnic basket. A bunch of rooks went flapping high overhead, cawing lazily to each other across the sky.

I looked up and down the platform. Chloe wasn't with me. Everything was empty, everywhere. There was only this basket on the platform, only last year's leaves, only the broken glass. The railway had stopped, the lines had all been taken up, the weeds and brambles had come in. The edge of the platform was crumbling away.

Chloe wasn't here.

I found myself running up the platform. I remember running back, stopping, looking all ways. I went from LUGGAGE to GENTLEMEN to WAY OUT. But the WAY OUT was to nowhere, the GENTLEMEN had rotted away, there was no place for LUGGAGE anymore. There was only our basket with the picnic.

My heart was thumping against my ribs. I found I was telling myself that of course Chloe could not be here, that she could never have been here, that I must have brought the picnic basket.

Yet it was then that I did catch sight of Chloe. She was all by herself on the other side of the track, out on the meadow, practising her slow cartwheels. She was going up sideways, staying up there, pointing her toes . . . and then coming very slowly down the other side.

She did them beautifully, unfolding herself like a fan, so that upside-down her hair poured golden from her inside-out skirt down into the grass, her bare legs stretched Y-high up above her in the sun. Then, with perfect mastery, she folded herself up again, tossing back her hair as her feet returned together on the ground. And then I watched her slowly turning back, unfolding round the other way.

Chloe was still with me.

I found myself snatching up our basket, jumping – almost falling – off the deserted railway platform, running back across the track towards her with a desperate relief!

9

'I'm starving,' Chloe announced.

Eagerly, I suggested that we should eat. Where we were would do. I would set it out. She seemed to like the idea of me getting it.

Chloe said: 'We could picnic on the station – under the shade of the canopy.'

But somehow, because she was coming, even that did not matter. Chloe let me sit her down on the edge of the platform while I got the picnic out all round her. I could not help but be amused, while I burrowed into the basket, at all the bits and pieces we had brought with us. No wonder it had been so heavy. It was obvious that she had been rather looking forward to us having all this. And it was not so much the food, which was ordinary enough as I remember, our freshly cut sandwiches and the plain apples and bananas and lemonade – it was the extras. I spread out the white cloth between us on the platform. There were two plastic glasses. There were two white paper serviettes. Chloe wanted it sort of formal. Not that I asked her at the time. I simply cottoned on. Looking back, I know it was exactly the right thing. Behind us were the still staring waiting-room windows, the shattered oil-lamp surrounded by its scattered glass, the doorless doorways looking down. But I could open the lemonade and pour out Chloe her drink. I could pass it across. She smiled as she accepted it from me.

'I'm famished,' Chloe said.

I sat there, watching her. Her red hair had fallen across her face. She was eating what was really one of my sandwiches, only I hadn't told her. For the first time she paused, mouth somewhat full, knees drawn up, feet on the cloth, her skirt full of crumbs.

'You're not talking again,' Chloe said.

I grinned at that.

I still could not see her face properly. She had put her face a little on one side as if she was waiting for a real reply back.

All at once – I can see myself doing it now – I got up, and carrying my plastic glass, I walked round the cloth and deliberately sat tight down beside her.

And then we both didn't speak. It was as if we were each waiting for the other one. At last I said it.

'Chloe – thank you for bringing me even this far.'

Her green eyes stared at me.

'It's been a marvellous morning,' she suggested. She in no sense moved away.

'No, it's not that Chloe. It's because you realise I know who you are and yet you've still brought me along.'

She had not quite expected that. For an infinitesimal moment her gaze shifted and then returned.

'Do you really know who I am, Matt?'

'I think so. But you tell me then. Say it out loud. I'd like you to tell me.'

She seemed to be considering my request.

'You know that I'm Chloe,' she said very simply.

Her face was terribly close. I was staring at a fascinating little pock mark set among the freckles between her eyebrows. I could see the minute down over the surface of her forehead.

'But I *really* know,' I told her. 'I *know* you're Chloe Tawney. You're the one they remember because she happened to get herself drowned in the weir. You're Tawney's daughter, the one who's dead. That's what they say. But you won't say.'

She seemed to think about it. Ever so slightly – she swayed.

'They – that's what they've told you?' she asked.

I nodded. With a rush I was declaring myself to be on her side. Though it was almost as if . . . she was not going to accept what I had said. Yet she did not in any way deny it. Only – it seemed as if I had to wait forever for her answer.

'Well?' Chloe said. And she sounded so curious. 'And what do you think?'

I reached up and took a strand of her red hair between my fingers. Now she did not move her head. I even ran my fingertips along her eyebrow and over that pock mark and down that nose. She let me – but she did not smile.

'They – they have told me that you're dead, Chloe – but you're not dead to me, are you? Are you? How can you be?'

She put my hand away from her face, but reluctantly, almost as if only to protect me.

'I – I am what you'd call dead, Matt. It's what I call – being otherwise. All I want is for you to talk about it with me. I want you to say what I am – find out what I'm like. All I want to do is to share it a little. And I promise I won't turn into something horrible or anything. It's not like having a disease. I'm much the same as I always was. Don't know what else to be – yet! Becoming otherwise happens to everybody'.

Yet she shuddered a little, she looked away from me.

'But Chloe – I can hear you. I can see you.'

'Don't you like seeing me?'

'Y-yes. But if you're . . . dead . . . I'm not supposed to see you.'

She picked up an apple. It was almost something to do. Yet I could see clearly that she understood.

'You can bend rules sometimes . . . sometimes it becomes

96

possible to see the otherwise. Shouldn't often happen. Usually, there's no need – we don't want to be seen.'

There was a hesitation in Chloe's voice as she told me, and yet an excitement as well, that she should be doing it at all. Perhaps I should not have listened. Perhaps we should have had no discussion. Yet between us, how could we have avoided . . . what she was?

'Chloe – why do *I* see you?'

'Starts with lots of reasons. Don't understand all of them. One is – I don't want to go on because I think my leaving was my fault. And another is because Tawney and Mum won't send me on – because they think it was all their fault. And at the same time they're afraid of me. Underneath I scare them – even Tawney – I scare the whole village. I never wanted to frighten. I don't blame them, not really. I know it's to protect themselves that they refuse to believe in me. It's as if they never wanted me to be born. They only want to think of me as nothing.'

I watched her as she crunched the apple. She looked so pale. I took hold of that strand of her hair a second time and, very gently so as not to hurt, I pulled at it so that she had to move her head a little.

'You don't seem to me like a nothing, Chloe.'

Again she put my hand away – but not in the least bit crossly. Rather, it was as if now I really knew, it gave me a chance not to touch her, as if I might not want to touch her.

'Matt – my mum even – when she sees me she won't look – even when I'm standing right in front of her. You've seen her do it. She won't admit that I'm here 'cause I'm supposed to be a nothing! She only wants to remember her own memories. Yet I am as I was. And 'cause I'm not supposed to be here everybody hates seeing me. They all insist I'm not here – except Tawney and now you. And Tawney only sees me 'cause he refused to admit that anything's ever different. And he doesn't really want me different. He wants to persuade himself that I never have died really. But I'm so tired of staying still. They none of them see me as learning and changing and wanting to go on. They none of them see me properly at all. It leaves me so lonely. And I know they still really love me . . . yet somehow they can only hurt me. My mum loves me! And I love them . . . but I have to go on hurting back! It just goes on and on and there never seems to be any way out.'

I could understand that. Already, this morning, I had been hurt, and she had not meant it.

'But Chloe . . . you still don't explain. I could never have known you before . . . yet I see you.'

The apple core was thrown down on the track.

'Wondered if you would. When I waited for your coach – thought you might not see me, 'cause to you I really would be a nothing. Even if you did see me, I thought, you might not have come with me. It was wonderful when you talked, when you walked back with me to the barn. I had only come out on the spur of the moment when I guessed Tawney had forgotten. Think it worked 'cause you knew my father so well, sort of knew him a bit like I did. And you didn't know anything about me so you couldn't be scared at first. Found that out from Tawney. Asked him if he had ever told you about me. He'd sort of wanted me to stay away. We had a row almost. That made my mind up. Then I got so afraid he'd stop you coming. I just wanted an ordinary friend.'

I can remember her saying that so earnestly . . . and I can remember at the same time so wishing that we could be ordinary.

'Do you – are you forced to go back to the weir then – over and over again? Is that what you have to do?'

Again Chloe waited – as if she was not sure how she could tell me, uncertain as to whether I would understand.

'In a way, Matt. I do have to. But also – it's my perform-

98

ance – the only one I've got. It's all people ever know about me now – me going back to the weir. Used to be – happy place really – even if, ever since I can remember, Mum was always warning me about it whenever we went. But we used to enjoy it. When I was small, she used to hold my hand. There's this narrow bridge across it and we used to stand there for ages looking at the water rushing and roaring away beneath our feet. I used to be bewitched just watching all the white foam going over its edge. We could never hear each other speak. Yet the water behind us, just before it went over, that always looked so smooth and still. There was a place on the other side where I liked to play. It was out of the wind. Sometimes Dad would find little harvest mice for me. He was good at those things. Sometimes he used to draw me. Mum and Dad agreed in those days and we really went up to the weir 'cause that was where he most liked to paint. We would often go out whole days for his painting. Never knew then what was going to happen there. I remember Mum trying awfully hard to stop Dad boring me by making me sit too long, when really she *had* taught me how to do it and I really *did* like sitting for him. It was always Mum who told me how good and patient I had been. Dad never bothered. It was Mum who always rewarded me with a piece of fudge at the end – but it was as if Dad got all the credit for it. Just as it was Mum who taught me to swim so well – because *she* can. If I was good at maths at school it was because Mum taught me how interesting it could be. But when I got the prize it was Dad I wanted to tell first.'

'Your mum –' I blurted out, 'she told me that Tawney won't go near the weir now.'

Chloe winced.

'That was after I went . . . after I drowned. He changed completely and yet he still wants to pretend that nothing really happened. Mum has tried to get him to go back, but he won't. Yet in the old days he was always painting at the

99

weir. If it wasn't me he would paint Mum. When Dad took us off to lonely places I didn't mind. It was when he wanted to paint me playing on the beach at Watermouth or somewhere that I hated it. People would crowd round to watch. At the weir though, there wouldn't be anyone else, 'cept Dad and Mum. I've always liked going there.'

I reflected that this was where we were now going to go. I remembered that I was to be her ordinary friend. We had moved a little away from each other now – and the odd thing was that this did not matter anymore. In some fashion we had both discovered that we could bear each other, at least for the moment. However dangerous our conversation might become we could continue this talking. I was only afraid of stopping talking.

'Chloe – did you like sitting for your father?'

'Not as much as Mum. She always felt she was doing something wonderful. So she was, for Tawney. She was always telling me, teaching me, how I was helping Dad. I didn't mind that much – p'raps sometimes I did – but it was fun to see what he made of me. Used to earn a Mars bar. And extra pocket money. And I always told him what I thought he'd done. Mum used to tick me off sometimes but Dad did listen.'

'Do you know, Chloe, they never told me why you went over the weir, the very first time.'

For a moment she stared down at the track beneath our feet as if wondering how to answer.

'Surely . . . surely they told you that I went over the Amberley weir twenty-five years ago 'cause I would swim where Mum told me not to! If they did – they were right. They told each other that I went over 'cause they weren't with me enough. P'raps they were right again. Now . . . the only thing that's supposed to be left is my new tomb in the church. I wanted you to see it 'cause it's Dad's design. Village didn't like it too much 'cause it reminded everyone of what had happened. It's as if people don't want to remember too much of what really does happen – but Tawney *would* do it like that, and they couldn't stop him. I like it. Yet you see, even though Dad made my tomb, he still won't face the fact that I've gone!'

She stopped talking then. I could hear the cuckoo, somewhere far behind us, somehow adding to the silence. My answer seemed so obvious, yet so cruel.

'But you haven't gone,' I told her softly. 'You keep coming back.'

'They won't let me go,' Chloe protested in a small indignant voice.

'You don't leave them,' I continued. 'You come back.'

'Do – d'you want me to go then?' Her face was almost angry.

'No. But I think you want to go.'

The silence hung endless on the warmth of the air. At long last Chloe looked round at me, gave a dumb nod.

'I just come back. I'm drawn back. You are right, Matt. I'm on a horrible sort of roundabout. It goes on and on and I go forward and back and can't change.'

'Chloe – where do you come back from?'

It was as if she had been stung. She drew away in sudden panic.

'Matt – you mustn't ever ask me that! It's too dangerous for you to know. You mustn't ever.'

'Why?'

'You mustn't even try to know.'

I can remember being surprised that I had so jolted her. But not only surprised . . . I became curious. And not only curious but somehow betrayed. She had been showing me her secret, sharing it with me, and now she wanted to stop short. We were trusting each other and now she did not want to trust me any further.

'Wouldn't I understand better if you tried to tell me?'

'It's too dangerous! Dangerous for you, Matt. Bad enough you being with me like this. You mustn't know where I *go* to. If I were to tell I might damage you like I damage every-one else I know. It's a question that ought to be forgotten – for your sake, Matt.'

The great meadow stretched away from our railway station, away and up as far as the eye could see toward the Amberley Mounds. I sipped the remains of my lemonade. Neither of us spoke.

At last I said: 'I'm sorry, Chloe.'

We met each other's gaze. Yet Chloe looked away from me, almost at once.

'I'm sorry too, Matt.'

But then the green eyes looked at me again – and I was startled to see how full of pain they were.

'Matt . . . if I said . . . if I told you . . . where I go . . . you would only learn to hate me. And I'd hate myself for doing it. Just as I hate myself everytime I find myself coming back. They tell me I can choose and yet I find myself returning over and over again. I come back. You should never have been told that I still go on. Just a part guess – that you don't quite believe in – that's all you should have. That would have been safe. But Matt, you know far too much already. You won't ever be able to stop asking questions. That's how I've betrayed you. You'll even hate me if I tell you that nobody would stay back here in your world, if only they knew. Your world's only funny shadows. When you're otherwise then everything's more real than here. D'you understand, Matt – it's *you* who are the ghosts. You're the cold ones. You're only spectres – just shadows waiting to begin. Only – you mustn't ever begin until you're ready. That's what's happened to me. I wasn't ready . . . I still can't get all of me to go on. Part of me stays here. That's what's so awful – I *am* otherwise but I can't *stay* otherwise.'

All at once she was on her feet, she had pulled away from me. She was walking down the deserted platform and I could hear her crying. Chloe was sobbing her heart out in the door-way where once the luggage went.

Everything else was so still. The sun beat down beyond the station canopy. Even the cuckoo was silent. I could see a trail of ants already marching on our table-cloth.

10

Together, or at least Chloe tried to help, we packed up the picnic, and we did not say too much. It was obvious that we were going on . . . we had to walk to the weir. But that was one thing we had not bothered to explain to each other. I felt that it had not been the thing to ask. Chloe knew that she had said too much already. Chloe was brave. To her, I think it was a relief to help me pack the basket; to me, I was glad to stand once more in the sun.

'Come on girl,' I said. 'Shake the cloth with me. Want to get the crumbs out of it.'

She picked up the other end. We could both see the expressions on each other's faces. We both knew that it wasn't crumbs we were thinking about.

'Only – only have to talk to me, Matt,' Chloe said in a rush. 'Or not talk to me, if that's how you happen to feel. Do walk with me, even if you do know what I am. Please don't go away.'

We shook the cloth together. We nodded with agreement at each other. Though Chloe did remind me that the cloth should be the last thing to go back in the basket. And she wanted to make quite sure that we did not forget anything. It was her suggestion that we buried the lemonade bottle instead of taking it with us. (I dug it down into the heap of ballast.) Then she had wanted to do her nails and I had lent her the nail file on my knife. I offered her my comb again, too. Though I did ask her who she thought we were going to see.

'You're going to see me,' Chloe pointed out.

When I got my comb back we wrangled over which of us would carry the picnic basket. She won – she carried it.

The railway track led on and up. We passed a stack of old sleepers left rotting in the bracken. At one place I even spotted lumps of coal, once spilled by some steam loco and now long embedded in the soil. There was still a sign – '19' – nineteen miles from the junction. The green meadow was narrowing, the line curved round into a forest of pines, silent, a trunk across our track, the pine needles under our feet. It was a long walk through muted grey shadow and under black branches. It was somehow solemn in there and we did not talk much . . . but Chloe did not complain. I noticed the birds did not sing there either. Only once was there an opening where the sunshine cascaded through and then Chloe simply pointed upward and I looked and there was a further towering mound across the valley. After that we were back within the forest, the grey gloom and the continual silence.

'Chloe?' I asked in an undertone.

'Yes,' she whispered back.

'Why did you go over the weir – the first time?'

'All so stupid. Started with Dad wanting to do this special picture and use me as his model and Mum wanting me to dance so that she could show me off at the Amberley Fair. They sort of forgot that I wanted to visit London, that I was trying to collect moths, that I was doing competition swimming down at Watermouth. S'pose I was selfish. But Dad's world was all his own in his work and Mum shared her life between Dad and the village. Apart from him she was always doing things for the community, never for a person. Village isn't everyone. Village isn't anyone. I discovered that. Village was really something in Mum's head. But I wanted to be something in Mum's head, too. And outside it. Now Mum thinks a ghost is a sort of disgrace to the village.

Prefers to pick marigolds and just stick them round my new tomb!'

'But Chloe, why did you go over the weir?' I persisted.

'It was an accident, Matt! It was a stupid accident and it was all my fault – not anybody else's. But I had swum the weir before. Of course I'd been told not to. Not only by Mum. Everybody said not. Right they were. But I had done it three or four times already. You have to swim hard, but if you do it doesn't take you down. You do get across. Did it! Had to try it when no one else was there, though. Couldn't ever get the boys to swim there. But I swam. One time I did it in the dark even. Just to prove I could. Took my things off this side, walked across the narrow bridge to the other side, swam back. D'you know it was standing there on the bridge, watching the water foaming and falling over and down under my feet that made me so scarey? Wasn't anyone about, of course. Just a few sheep. Wind was a bit cold. The bridge only had one rail – to hold on to. But I made myself stop and look, and then look again. Made myself walk on over and then swim back. Wasn't any sun to sit in after, either.'

I stared at her with a kind of appalled admiration.

'But Chloe, why did you have to do it?'

'Just for – just – 'cause I had to do it! I don't know why.'

'So – if you could swim it – what made you go over?'

We walked . . . we walked for some distance before Chloe replied.

'It wasn't night at all. Lovely afternoon really. I had got angry. Mum wanted me to go with her to this do at Lower Spilcombe. Lady Somebody was going to open their flower show and we were going to do the folk dancing. Mum was in the middle of all the arrangements, as usual, even though it wasn't our village. Mum always is. She wanted me to wear an awful new dress I didn't like, and it was the wrong length, and we had a row. And I'd sat for Dad in the morning and he had hardly talked to me and had got angry with his own

106

work, which was hardly my fault. So I walked out on Mum and refused to go. Mum had to go. I was steaming cross and I walked and walked to the weir. The weir was a favourite, private place. I was going to swim just to annoy Mum – even if it wouldn't really annoy her because she wouldn't know! She was annoyed enough anyway. Or I'd tell her! Yes, I'd tell her what I did during the flower show. Then I undressed. As soon as I'd done it I had this silly impulse to put it all on again – everything, even the shoes – and swim across like a lady. I'd lady 'em! And it would spoil the dress – dry clean only! Remember reading the label. Must have been mad. Yet somehow, it was exciting going into the water all dressed up. I so knew I was a good swimmer, and it wasn't until I got out into the middle that I found that I couldn't swim quite so well, not with all that on. It took me some time to realise that I wasn't going to be able to swim faster than the current, that it was taking me and that there was no escaping. I remember that I didn't even panic. All seemed so inevitable. I had made a mistake. Found myself deliberately taking what I thought was to be my last look at the sunshine while I was being banged from side to side . . .'

I could not reply. I hung on to the fact that she could not, would not, tell me anymore; that that was the end, that there wasn't anything else to say.

'It was funny – there wasn't any pain. Only a long long time when I knew nothing. It seemed like days when I only knew a sort of ringing blankness. And then . . . when I saw again . . . I did not understand anything. Only that nothing hurt. I never felt anything. Only I knew that I ought to have been in agony and I felt so perfect – and it was wrong. It was like being free and there being no point in having any freedom . . .' Her voice trailed away. For some steps she walked on in silence. 'But then I'm not supposed to talk about that,' she whispered.

'We're not going to talk about it,' I assured her. 'I'm only coming to the weir because it's a marvellous place to see, because your father liked to do a lot of his work there. If that's what you want.'

Chloe glanced gratefully across at me.

'Just want you to come with me,' she said.

The pine needles lay thick where the railway once had been.

At length the track ahead began to come clear of the forest, the trees started to thin out, the sunlight began to come through. The railway was coming out high on the side of a new valley. I touched her on the arm.

'Wait for me a sec,' Chloe. 'Must go behind a tree while there's still one left.'

She did not seem to quite cotton on.

'Why?'

'You silly old idiot! Why d'you think?'

'Oh . . . you won't go far? You aren't just going to walk away from me, are you? You won't not come back?'

'You're still a silly old idiot,' I assured her.

From where I eventually stood I found that I could still just see her down across the bracken. She waited there, in the middle of the track, quite a little way below me, standing in that inconsequent way people do when they just wait, holding our basket, shifting her weight idly from one foot to the other.

It was somehow marvellous that she should be waiting there for me.

Back in the sun we began to quicken our step. A certain air of excitement was beginning to come over Chloe.

'Steam engines used to make an awful fuss coming round this bit,' she told me.

I was careful not to make any fuss. Far below now I could see the steep-sided valley between the Mounds and then, as we completely rounded our side, I could see that our track led straight over it across a viaduct. There were five curving stone arches with a river wriggling down through the lofty centre arch.

'Getting down's easier on the other side,' Chloe said.

I could see that getting down was going to be quite a business. So was getting across. The single-track viaduct had no real walls or parapets. It went like a ruler for over 500 yards before it got to the other side. They hadn't bothered to remove the old railway lines off the viaduct either.

'C'mon!' Chloe called over her shoulder.

She began running over the sleepers ahead of me. I followed, more gingerly, carrying the picnic basket, walking down the middle of the old rusting track, the sun full on me, walking sleeper to sleeper. By the time she had got to the middle of the viaduct Chloe must have realised that I was not with her for she stopped and waited.

I was walking further and further away from the real ground, my feet going from one old sleeper to the next, and somehow I felt I had no sides . . . I could only . . . sense somehow . . . the tree-tops in the valley underneath. I would not take two and a half steps to either side and then go over; yet there was a hot and uncomfortable sense on the back of my neck that there was absolutely nothing to prevent me doing it.

I went on walking.

'Look Matt,' she called. She was pointing. 'There it is.'

But I was not looking to where she was pointing. All I could see was that she was stepping forward, that she was standing outside the rails, outside the sleepers and on the very edge.

Chloe's toes clutched round the edge of the viaduct brickwork.

I stopped still.

'Chloe – be careful,' I said. I tried to say it softly, terrified that by simply speaking to her . . .

'I don't have to be careful.'

I stared at her. For she was so unconcerned. Yet there was

nothing, nothing but the balance of her own body, between her and the reeling space down to the green valley floor. I had to put the picnic basket down. Just – just to manage to look, it was a peep and to do that I had to kneel on the rusting track, and even then I felt cold and gooey.

'But I – I have to be careful,' I said. 'I'm sorry.'

And then all at once she had realised and she had stepped back and was crouching on her heels beside me, her breath in my ear.

'Oh Matt – I forget – it's me that ought to be sorry. It's just what I shouldn't do. Look – can you bear to see?'

Chloe had to point before I could look, her face beside mine, her hair across my eyes, and only then did I realise what she wanted me to see.

I saw the river flowing through the water meadow far below, flowing between willows, bending to the left and widening to a sort of basin. It was like a small lake. On the far side there was a wall with a gap and a footbridge across it. Below the bridge there was an edge. It was only when I saw that edge that I heard the sound of distant roaring and knew what I was looking at.

It was the sound of many tons of water pouring.

'The weir,' I croaked.

'Doesn't look very much, does it? Doesn't look anything. It's the way I went. I went alone. That's why I want you to come down with me. That's why I want to show it to you. I want to share it a little. It's become all mine, my property . . . and I don't want it. I want to be rid of it.'

She was holding on to me, I could feel her shaking, but I could only hold on to the rail, cling on to it and not say anything, frozen in the sun by where I was and what was happening.

'I'm so alone, Matt – so alone for so long. I'm trapped between where I was and where I'm going. Can't reach back or forward. D'you know – just now – had to stop myself. Be so easy – too easy – just to pull you a little – just for both of us to go over. So like to take you – but it would do no good! I know it would do no good. You would end up like me. It would be too early. Until you have lived in your world the next is no good. It's only living here that lets you understand it there. I went too soon – far too soon! That's what's happened to me. P'raps it wouldn't be so bad for you. You've got things you want to do. People think you can do things. You've begun. But only when I've come to understand – and I don't know when or how – only when I can forgive Mum and Tawney and myself, only then shall I be able to begin and can stop returning and returning.'

I took a deep cold breath. I could see from her face that she meant so exactly what she said. And I felt afraid so differently . . . at once so afraid for the Chloe I had come to know . . . and at once, most terrible of all . . . I felt, as I looked down over this sunny green void with its bright river, this edge to the leafy tree-tops beneath us, an enormous growing curiosity.

'Chloe,' I said. It might have been an exclamation, it might have been a question, I might have been going to tell her – tell her what? Perhaps she was stronger than me. It wouldn't even be my fault. She had all the advantages. I could feel her fingers round my arm and I could begin to sense myself wanting her to do it. She had only to push – to pull me so gently.

Yet suddenly she had let go of me, she was staring at me, had jumped back from me so that now she was sitting on her heels in the middle of the sleepers, her hands gripping the rails, as if she too had become afraid of the viaduct.

'C'mon! Let's get to the other end, Matt. D'you hear it? Down below us? That's the Amberley river, going over. When I hear it, it echoes in me! Over and over again . . . it's always going. It still hurts – changing worlds – and I have to keep changing so often and often. But they both call, they both hurt, wherever I am. I must go down.'

Chloe stood up. I found it difficult getting on to my feet.

I was shuddering too. I couldn't take her hand. I couldn't take the basket. Chloe seemed to understand this for she took the basket from me and didn't laugh. She just walked on ahead. I knew I couldn't walk the other way. I knew I could not leave her. It would have been too cruel to have left her then. I did not want to leave Chloe. Yet if I was honest with myself I also knew that I was not really choosing. I tottered after her, over the wooden sleepers, looking neither left nor right, telling myself over and over again not to, telling my feet only to walk.

Almost at the end, and I was praying to get to that end, to get off this viaduct. Chloe maddened me by stopping.

'See the foam where the water slops over? D'you see where it goes mostly through the centre?'

I didn't. I didn't want to. Yet even then I did not want Chloe to see me not wanting to see.

Chloe skipped on ahead. I just walked to the end of this viaduct, just walked on to its end. Just to put my foot down on soft soil again was like lifting a black curtain. I stood still.

She was waiting for me. She stood there, wrinkling up her freckled nose. The green eyes looked at me, they were concerned, I suppose they told me I was important.

'Thank you for coming, Matt,' she said all over again.

'Thank you for asking me.'

We sounded absurdly formal. Yet it was not absurd. I took hold of her hand. It was hot. Or mine was cold. We smiled. We giggled at each other like a pair of fools. We wrestled, we gripped hold of each other rather carefully and rolled over on the grass. We both knew we were not wrestling to fight but because it was a kind of conversation. When we stopped we sat apart from each other as if to think over what we had said.

11

We had left the disused railway. The roaring of the water was not so far away now. As we picked our way down the valley side it became more insistent . . . not enough to make it in any way difficult to talk . . . yet all the time it told me that we were coming to this one particular place.

The going down was almost easy. I went first and it was a zigzag path down through the bracken and the roots of the trees were like steps. One caught glimpses of dragonflies. Spider-webs touched at one's mouth, one's face. At times we were almost waist-deep in the bracken and here and there it was slippery underfoot. Once I had to grab at a tree-trunk. Further down I had to grab at Chloe as she slithered by me. We had to concentrate so hard on our feet that it was quite a shock to look up and discover that the viaduct arches were now curving high above our heads. We had to jump a small stream at the bottom and pick up the path again where it ducked beneath the green trailers of a weeping willow. All at once we had come out beside the Amberley river, rock and grassy slopes and overhanging trees. It widened quite a way across.

'This is where we should have picnicked,' I said.

'Didn't want to talk about this place *at* this place, Matt. And everything was different then – before the picnic.'

We had stopped at the edge of the river-bank. I wondered what she was going to do. The water seemed so dark here under the willows and it moved so swiftly. It was smooth and if you did not look carefully you might almost have thought that it was still. But then all at once you would see a leaf, a twig, a feather go sweeping by.

Only we stood still.

I could see that the river led up to a long straight line, to a low stone wall. In the centre of the stone wall was the gap, a gap with its narrow footbridge over, a bridge hardly wider than a gang-plank and with a single rail. Under the bridge was an edge of water. It was from the edge of water that the river roared.

Chloe watched me.

'This is the place,' she said flatly.

'The weir?'

'The weir is the way I have to go.'

She must have read my face because she went on.

'Sometimes I stay here for days, sometimes a day or only half a day. Then I have to go. Have to go the way I went the first time. It calls me. I have to. It never quite stops calling whatever I do here. Sometimes it is only a distant murmur, other times it asks me, many times I am told, and I have to come here, whatever I am doing.'

'Do you mean – then you have to go – over the weir?'

Chloe nodded.

'What is so stupid is that I am more frightened now than on that first day . . . although now I have done it often and often. D'you know I've never told Tawney I have to come here. I could never have told my mum. Yet the story goes round in the village that I come. S'pose I've been seen, one time and another. I've tried not to be seen. But it's lonely by oneself – going over. Never ever anyone to say good-bye to me when I was called, never anyone who could have said good-bye to me – before. I've so often had to go. So I thought, if ever I did have the courage to tell you who or what I was – that you might just come and see. Can you bear to?'

I could not help but look at the gap in the wall where the water roared, tipped, endlessly, relentlessly down to the level below. It took time for her words to make meanings in my head.

'After you met me – off the coach – you had to come here?'

'No. I have been here since you came here. But I know I must go on in a little while.'

'Are – are you going now?'

'In a little while. When I am ready.'

'Do I – won't I see you again? You're – you're not going for ever now, are you?' All at once it gripped me, what she was doing.

'Dead people shouldn't come back. I'm not supposed to come back. But I'm tied to coming back. Might come back tomorrow. May have to come back. Want to see you again – oh, over and over again. Yet I want to go on, Matt. I so long to go on. Say you'll say good-bye to me today.'

I am not sure that, at the time, I fully understood. I only understood that she was unhappy.

'Of course I will say good-bye. But I would rather say hello. And if you do come back tomorrow . . .'

Chloe turned away from the river as if to look back down the way we had come. There were the tall arches of the viaduct like high narrow windows on the valley up behind.

'Always had to come back. Always will 'til I believe I can go on. Only half a being over there. Can't let go – of this place. I take too much with me. Or I take the wrong things. No one tells me what the right things are. There was always my mum to tell me before, even if I did not always agree with her. She could always make things work. She could always show me how to make things work. But she couldn't show me how to die. How could she have guessed that I would have been such a fool? And she was always so patient with me. I could always ask her again and again and she would always reshow me. Dad used to get cross if I got cold or stiff sitting for him. And now I can't be patient with my mum or help her back – even though she needs me. I can't begin to talk to her.'

I put my hand on her arm. Yet I saw myself walking the long way back along the disused railway to Tawney's barn, alone. But I saw Chloe too, walking there, time after time . . . and time after time coming back here after leaving her father, her mother . . . and nobody really understanding why she was there at all. I did not understand. Yet I knew that I had become used to her, here and today. I simply liked her being here – and now that she was going to go away – she was not going to be here. I wanted her to walk all the way back with me. I wanted her to be not in any particular hurry, just talking of this and that. I wanted to go to sleep knowing that I would talk to her tomorrow.

Even then I kept forgetting what she was.

She was watching me.

'This is where I swam from on that afternoon. Always have to swim from here now. This place.'

'Chloe – what will you want me to do – to say good-bye?'

For a moment she did not answer. She even turned aside and began to hunt around in the picnic basket. She dug about in there for what seemed an awfully long time. I could not see what she was looking for – at? Then at last she actually fished up a comb of her own and sat back on her heels to do her hair.

'Do, Matt? Just – just stand here and watch me swim out there – until you can't see me anymore. Wave to me, even if I can't see you waving. And be sorry that I'm going and be glad that I was here. Could you, Matt? Wish I could take you with me . . . or that I could really stay. But you must not come and I cannot stay.'

I nodded. She could see from my face that of course I would wish her good-bye, if that was what she wanted me to do. But inside I didn't think saying good-bye was anywhere near enough.

She combed out her red hair so carefully. There was still a streak of dirt on her face from the waiting-room and on an impulse I wet my hand in the river and came back and wiped it off. Chloe smiled, put out her tongue at me, went on combing.

'Chloe, when you come back to us, do you arrive here?'

'No. Always arrive at the cottage where Mum lives, where we all used to live, by the Rectory. My room's still there. S'not changed much. It's my room – where I always come back. That's where I open my eyes. My clothes have all gone now. Used to have a blue teddy-bear called Glubb. Mum's chucked him. Think my wellingtons were the last to go. Mum didn't notice them on top of the wardrobe. But it's still my room. To me – it's where I always come back. Yet I come here – when it's time to go on.'

'Aren't you – aren't you tired of all these journeys?'

'Not tired, Matt. I can't be tired. Being tired doesn't happen now. But frightened – I'm always frightened of coming – in case Mum and Tawney aren't here anymore – so there wouldn't be anywhere to go on from. Yet this frightens me – going on over the weir. You see I'm not even sure who *is* going on. And that's worse than all the bumping. Nothing ever seems to be for the better. Today's the best day I've ever had, Matt. Just talking to you.'

She bunged the comb back into the basket.

I looked down at her kneeling back on her heels in the grass, her jersey all grubby, her cotton skirt marked and creased from the walk, from Little Oaken Station, from coming down the bank. I certainly knew who she was. I had met her, eaten with her, got things for her, waited for her.

'Chloe, if you can't talk to your mum – why don't you tell Tawney? You talk to him! Tell him you don't know who you are.'

An agonised look came over her face as she looked at me.

'*I can't!* He's got to find out. It's got to come from him. It's no good if it doesn't come from him. Yet I don't know what to do, Matt. He doesn't even try to find out now.

P'raps – p'raps he's frightened of me. But I can't say. All I do is just go on and on like this and find out less and less. Everything's all slipping away. But what else can I do except come back?'

'You could do something for me, Chloe. Would you?'

She gaped at me.

'Tell me what I can do, Matt.'

'Two things,' I said. 'First one will be easy for you. Do me – do me a couple of cartwheels.'

Unexpectedly, she laughed.

'That is two things, Matt.'

'One thing,' I insisted. 'You can. I've seen how you can. Do me two cartwheels.'

She saw that I really meant it. For a moment she stood there, motionless, trying to decide why I should want her to. She seemed amused, flattered, puzzled . . . even a little shy. Then all at once she made up her mind, walked away, turned her back towards me – and turned them.

She turned them, first the one way and then the other. She could do them with a wonderful kind of lazy elegance, her feet pointing across the sky, one leg seeming so slow to follow the other, her hair sweeping the grass and then perfectly she was standing upright once again. And then she leaned the other way and it was as if the world turned and she hung still. Twice she made herself both inside-out and upside-down.

'Am I any good?' Chloe wanted to know.

'You're a lot of good,' I told her.

'Well, if that's only one thing – what's the other?'

'You may not like me asking,' I said cautiously.

'I'll do it if I can. Is it going to be difficult?'

'It won't be difficult. Not for you. But it may be the last thing you will do. I know you won't do it for Tawney.'

'Won't do it for Tawney? What won't I ever do for Tawney?'

'Not that I could ever do his bit of it as well as he can. And

I haven't brought any of my stuff with me anyway. But I still want to ask you.'

'Oh Matt, you are making a lot of mysteries.'

'Can't you remember Chloe, that I really came down here to see your dad? He was going to teach me a bit. He'd promised to give me a whole week of drawing lessons. So this is the second thing I'm asking. I only want you to sit down – just there.'

She did not quite know how to take me. She opened her mouth to protest – or to laugh – or to be pleased – and then shut it again. I shall never know which it was. Chloe sat.

I sat too.

'I'm going to look at you,' I said. 'I haven't got a pencil and I haven't got a sketch-book. But Tawney's been asking me to move an imaginary pencil in my head. So that's what I'm doing. And it's you that's sitting. I know you got fed up sitting for your dad, but this time you're sitting for me. That's what I'm asking you to do. And for you it won't make any difference that I am not putting pencil on paper. Sitting will be the same. And what I do for me isn't so important as what you are doing for you – sitting!'

'Don't mind sitting for you. Wish you really were drawing me.'

'But I really am looking at you. Go on – turn your head a little more that way . . . I can see your left ear coming out through your hair. And the way your nose tips up at the end. Now the smile's coming round. No – I'm being serious – please don't giggle – well, all right – you laugh, it changes the shape of your chin.'

(But she was also a shape against a willow tree and the bracken. Light against the bark of the tree, the light of her hair, the pale of her face. That's how I could have made the pale show up. At least I was being able to look at her as if I had been drawing – and looking is always what the drawing is all about. And Chloe was not any girl. She did take me

119

perfectly seriously. I remember those lines coming up between her eyebrows.)

'You're sitting back with your palms flat down on the grass and your feet stretched out in front of you. I can see the dirt lines on the soles of your feet. No – don't pull your feet up. You can wriggle your toes, if you like.'

'Now you're not being serious,' she complained, very seriously. 'Perhaps I should move more if you're planning a drawing. Give you all the choices. If I do bring my knees up then how I sit all changes, doesn't it?'

I nodded.

'You know as much about it as I do, don't you Chloe? You've sat for Tawney so often . . . You must have picked up all sorts of things about him . . . Learnt how to be a real model. You never sit awkwardly or too tight, do you?'

'Dad was fond of saying that Chloes never sat too tidy. Mum was different. Always had to look scrubbed and tidy for Mum. But she could teach you how to dance. She said I was easy to teach and maybe I was. But Mum could make the most hopeless people do it. Sure I never could. She was always so patient with them.'

'. . . and knees are difficult. There's not much to go on with a knee, but if you get it wrong it all goes wrong. But then, Chloe – you are good at swimming too, aren't you. I mean, you *could* swim across the weir, in the ordinary way. However stupid it was, you did do it, when others couldn't.'

'Trouble was, Matt – I thought it was important and nobody else did – or were too busy. And now I know that it wasn't a bit important and that it was stupid.'

She was standing up on the tips of her toes and then slowly crouching down so that I could watch her knee-caps move. She even turned round so that I could see the backs of her knees too. Backs of knees aren't easy either.

Chloe looked round at me over her shoulder.

'Me?' she asked shyly.

'You,' I told her.

'Am I why – am I why you wanted me to do cartwheels?'

I ran a forefinger between the tendons on the back of her knee. She let me.

'That's how – that's how you told me who you were. Can't you feel it – even now, can't you feel it?'

The water roared on over the weir beyond her.

I remember her sitting on her heels in front of me, her green eyes searching my face from less than a foot away, and yet not saying anything to me, not saying a word.

I stared back.

All at once she jumped up and did me a whole row of cart-wheels across the grass.

I can see her now, almost excited, standing on the edge of the bank with her back to the Amberley river. And then she had to walk up and down. When she stopped she stood first on one leg and then on the other.

'Have to swim, Matt. Being called. I've – I've got to go on. You will say good-bye still? Want to come back to-morrow to see you again. Want to look at your sketch-book – if you'll let me. But I'm being called first. Being called awfully strong. P'raps nothing's different – but I have to go on to find out. I can't – can't stay here.'

I could understand that she could not stay and yet I felt myself stepping out into some cold sensible unbearable misery. It was as if I had just reached across to her – and she was being snatched away. I did not want . . .

'Chloe – shall I wave to you from the bridge? I could wave to you so much longer from there.'

'Oh please, Matt. But you must be quick. I – I shall have to plunge in – in a minute. Please run Matt, run for me. I shan't be able to stop myself.'

She sat down. She stood up. She licked her lips and kept tossing back her hair. I wanted to go up and kiss her, hold her hand, put arms round her . . . But there was no time anymore.

'See you tomorrow, Chloe.'

She hugged herself. She marked time with her feet. She bent forward almost as if she was in pain.

'Hope tomorrow, Matt.'

I ran.

I carried the picnic basket as I ran. I knew that I could not have kissed her or said a proper good-bye or anything. I only asked myself if I had helped her or just made matters worse. I supposed that it wasn't really my business. But what else could I have done? I ran like mad.

Standing there on the slippery narrow cat-walk the roar of the water was overwhelming. If it had not been for Chloe I don't think I could have stood there. You see, the bridge was hardly three feet above the lip of the weir but from over the lip one could see the water foaming and falling to nearly fifteen feet below. I had only one greenish rail to hang on to. The cat-walk was made of wooden slats and I could see the water swirl beneath. Everywhere there was a spray so that my face, legs, clothes – everything was soaked.

I waved.

Chloe looked so far away. She was still back there on the bank, sitting crouched now, her hands locked round her knees as if to keep herself still. She jumped up when she saw my wave. All at once she was released. She did not have to resist anymore. One hand waved back . . . She made a powerful racing dive into the Amberley river, fully clothed.

For an instant I wondered why she had not stripped off and then, with a cold pang, remembered that all this was happening because she had insisted on swimming across the river fully dressed.

I watched. She swam a distinctly stylish crawl. Surely she could get across. She hadn't any shoes on. She wasn't wearing all that much at all. Yet something in Chloe herself steered her inexorably towards me, towards this roaring edge of the weir. It was very frightening. I saw her red hair spread out over the water behind her. I did not know if she could see me. But I waved, I waved madly.

And then it all happened because I glanced behind. I saw the water crashing down below. Chloe would never hear my shout. I also saw the top of the weir wall, just below me, just below the surface.

Chloe was coming. She had stopped swimming. Her face looked up at me, a hand was waving back, but it was a despairing face, she was coming with a terrible swoop under my feet.

I dropped flat on my tummy.

I simply could not stop myself. The roaring was in my ears. Chloe was going to go over and I could not bear it.

Holding on with one hand I clutched down with the other – I grabbed at Chloe's hair. I got it and did not let go. She was swept hard against the wall by the force of the water but I had stopped her going over. My feet managed to get a grip on the slats of the cat-walk. Somehow I managed to get a hand under her arm. I think she was screaming. I thought that for one awful endless instant I was going over with her, that we were both going to pitch down over the edge in each other's arms. I remember hanging upside-down over space and spray and the plummetting falling river. I shall never know how I got her back up on to the bridge. She fought me, then helped me, then I must have fainted.

I remember opening my eyes on a calm blue sky. I was lying in bracken and someone was bending over me. I could hear the sound of the weir but it now seemed very far away.

I was being asked, over and over again, if I was going to be all right.

I did not take too much notice at first. It did not seem to be of much importance. I tried, in a vague sort of way, to piece together everything that had happened. It was almost as if I was myself standing apart and watching myself coming-to. It even came as a sort of revelation to me that this person bending over me should be Chloe.

'Do, do say something, Matt,' she was pleading.

Her hair hung in rat's tails and dripped down on me. Her jersey and pants clung wetly to her. I had some sort of memory that she had lost her skirt getting back up on to the cat-walk. I only knew now that she should not have come back. That it was all due to my sudden, stupid idiocy that she was *here*. And over and over again she was asking *me* if I was all right!

I had stopped her going on.

I blurted out that I was sorry. I realised that she must hate me. I should not have done it but I had not been able to help it. I said that I just hadn't been brave enough simply to stand there and let her slide over, to let her go. I told her that I had not wanted her to go.

She knelt down beside me as if to hear what I was trying to say. I just lay there listening to myself babbling my own nonsense. I can remember staring up at the droplets of water standing out on the freckles of her face, even on her eyelids, on the bridge of her nose. The water went on dripping down on me from the ends of her hair. I was realising that she must have equally rescued me. But what so amazed me was how pleased she was to hear me speak.

'Shan't – couldn't ever hate you, Matt. You only wanted to save me. Taught me that I've always wanted to be saved – even though I've long been otherwise. That's something I've never realised properly until now. You see, on that silly afternoon when I first went over, when it all happened, I knew perfectly well that Tawney and Mum couldn't possibly be there. Yet somehow I had always expected them to rescue me at the last moment. I've always resented the fact that they weren't there! Yet how could they have been? But for so long now I've still gone on feeling that they should have been there. Until this time. This time, you were there.'

Her voice sounded perfectly clear and yet I can remember

being convinced that it came from a very long way away. Yet I could feel the bracken under me, the sun's warmth, my own clothes clinging to me. I sat up a little. It seemed that I had not quite done the wrong thing.

'. . . long as you're all right, Matt. You tried so hard for me. Sorry if I winded you. You have the knack of doing all the right things.'

I told her that now I had no idea what to do.

'Poor Matt. You've got the hardest thing of all yet.'

I saw that she was excited – concerned too – but bubbling over underneath.

'Don't you understand, Matt – I shan't have to come back, not anymore. Shan't have to go on by going over the weir – I'm freed of all that – thanks to you. I can go on, at last. This is the end of being half here. I can change. I've become free – but the first thing I have to do is to hurt you – have to ask you to put up with me hurting you, by going away. Because I'm free – I can't choose anymore – I have to go.'

But I did not understand then. I had to tell her that she was sopping wet, that we had to get her dry and home. I only made her laugh.

'Don't you see it doesn't matter – not where I'm going. I have to go where it is always otherwise and always home. Funny, isn't it – you've helped me to go on because you wanted me to stay. You keep forgetting what I am, don't you? Perhaps I forget it too. But it means being more real. Waited so long to be properly real. Waited so long to let go.'

Even then, her words did not fully penetrate. Looking back, possibly she had already begun to go though I had not realised. I asked her what I should tell her mother – and Tawney. I did not know what to tell myself.

'They'll know. Say – say thank you for me. Not any special message. Mustn't be any special message. I've talked too much anyway.'

I think it was a little later, when I was watching her squeezing the water out of her hair, twisting it like a red rope, her back turned to me, her head down, it was then that I knew that she was going for ever. I opened my mouth and shut my mouth and could only say nothing.

'You didn't half pull,' she was telling me. 'Thought my head would come off when you grabbed for me.'

I managed to smile a little.

'Don't forget the picnic basket,' she reminded me. 'Tawney's always using it on his expeditions. Hangs up behind the kitchen door.'

I told her I would not forget. I did not say to her that I did not want her to go – that I could not bear her to go. I did not say that I was sitting there wishing that I had not helped at all. I knew that it was a stupid wish – and went on wishing it.

'Matt?' she was asking.

'Mmmmmm?'

'Will you promise not to make fun of me if I take these wet things off? You won't laugh?'

I did not quite know why but I found myself more alarmed than laughing.

'I expect you're getting cold, aren't you?' I tried to sound full of common sense.

'Not that. It's that I can't take anything with me now. Mustn't take any of your world with me. Mustn't take anything with me 'cept myself.'

It was then that I knew that she was going further away than I could ever imagine.

'I shan't laugh at you. But are you sure you want me to be here?'

'Please stay, Matt. If you don't mind. Just to be here and to say good-bye, to see me go and know that I've gone.'

She turned away, tugged off her things and dropped them in the grass. She was a little awkward over it, perhaps because they were so wet. Even without them she still looked a bit goosey, a bit like a drowned rat. She came back and stood in the sun, the mass of freckles about her shoulders and midriff, her dark red hair, yet although she stood so close to me she seemed already to be further away.

'I – I wanted to draw you like that, Chloe. But I would never have had the courage to ask.'

Chloe nodded, she appeared to half hear, she appeared to listen and to understand.

I struggled up on to my feet. I was still shaky. My ears were still full of the roar of the weir. Looking at it, the surface of the river still seemed so motionless. The green Mounds of Amberley stood high above us, the forgotten railway hung over our heads. I would have to find all my own way back.

'How – how are you going on?' I ventured to ask.

'I'll just go. No – don't come any nearer to me. You mustn't touch me now. I want to wish you so well. Want you to remember me. Want you to remember an ordinary girl you just happened to meet. That's what I am. As others are – so I was. As I am – so will they be. You must not be sorry for me for being what I am. Only sorry that we shan't see each other. It is good where I go. And good not to come back. Good for everyone. Say good-bye for me. Say good-bye to me and watch me go. I shall go far away but I shall remember. No, stay where you are. Only . . . only say good-bye.'

I think I can remember my own voice saying that good-bye. But what I remember more clearly is Chloe herself, standing there in the green bracken, her feet a little apart, her hands on her hips, looking away from me . . . and waiting. Yet I am certain that it was I who sent her away. It was as if my attention faltered, as if my watching attention had become unable to hold her together. Her freckles became dots of brown, she became a splurge of red lost in the green and the grey of the river, in the touches of blue. She, her hair, her face, her shape, became streak and line and spot. What I had known as Chloe did not go away but became otherwise.

127

Chloe had become marks made across my mind. What had once made Chloe raised a hand within my head and waved.

Mr. and Mrs. Tawney came over the grass, towards me, together. Their relief at finding me was obvious. The way they came towards me – I might almost have been Chloe. I must have looked very shocked and stunned.

'She – she won't come back again. She'll never come back now.'

For a long time I did not say anything more.

They had brought some things with them. They were very kind. They made me drink something. I can hardly remember what they said. I have an odd memory of part of me being quite happy and yet the tears came streaming down my face. Not that it mattered with them. It did seem an endless way back and we all went to their first cottage, the one by the Rectory. That night of my holiday we all stayed there. I slept in Chloe's old room.